They left that basement and walked uptown in the dimness of daybreak. The streets were a deserted mess. Cars stopped in traffic with no one in them. Newspapers and trash flying around. Smashed windows on the storefronts. And silence. Their footfalls echoed off the tall buildings. Behind the gray clouds it was speckly, like a monitor screen gone wrong. A small green dot hovered up there. Adrian watched it for a while as they walked until it blipped out of existence.

Whenever they heard something or saw something move, they hid. Abandoned storefronts, an old wreck of a house, and alleyways all made good hiding places. Something moved. It could have been anything. It could even have been someone who was still normal. Antoine wasn't taking any chances with Adrian's life. So they took cover and waited for whatever it was to pass.

Things fell apart so fast. Who would have guessed that the city could look this way so soon after the incident? That's what their dad called it, the Incident. He seemed pained even saying that much. Now their dad was gone. But Adrian had Antoine. He was going to look out for him. He would always look out for him.

ELYSIUM

Or, The World After

Jennifer Marie Brissett

Aqueduct Press, PO Box 95787
Seattle, WA 98145-2787
www.aqueductpress.com

ISBN: 978-1-61976-053-0
Copyright © 2014 by Jennifer Marie Brissett
First printing, December 2014

Library of Congress Control Number: 2014947864
10 9 8 7 6 5 4 3 2 1

Cover illustrations: "Road to Dead City" © Can Stock Photo Inc / rolffimages; "Elk" © Can Stock Photo Inc/Almaviva
Interior illustration: Feather © Sasha1610/ Shutterstock.com

Book and Cover Design by Kathryn Wilham

Poem (p. 85) from "NGH WHT" in *The Dead Emcee Scrolls* by Saul Williams reprinted with permission of Simon & Schuster. Copyright © 2006 Saul Williams.

Printed in the USA by Thomson-Shore, Inc.

The flutter flutter of death's wings came for my beloved,
but I was not ready to let go...

```
>>
>> open bridge
Connecting...

*BRIDGE CONNECTED*
>>
>>
>> begin program

BRIDGE PROCESS: INITIATED 0000-00-00 00:00
    .
    .
    .
```

1.

Floating high above the city, dipping and swooping through the valleys of cinderblocks and concrete, landing on the edge of a rooftop to look down upon the inhabitants below. Watching, seeing, learning. They walk along the streets, alleys, and avenues. Moving here, going there, in a constant state of rush. Appointments to be kept, people to see, things to do. And Adrianne was one of them. She had somewhere to go. It was not deathly important. Just something she had been looking forward to all week, lunch with a friend at a place where they could sit by a window and watch the beautiful ones pass, examine their clothes, and take notes while rolling noodles around their forks, pretending to eat.

The city was a place to both love and despise. A place where a patchwork of new and old gray buildings stood side by side with icy-glass-covered skyscrapers. A blended terrain of high and low structures, each bookmarking history. A place Adrianne called home. She could never see herself leaving, though she often wondered how she could remain. Her mind wandered on so many useless thoughts as she walked along the busy sidewalk. Then she noticed, among the cars and the trucks and the buses, an elk. Its furry hindquarters protruded as it entered the crowd and sauntered through the shoppers, the vendors, and the construction workers. Its antlers rose high upon its elegant head, spreading upwards like giant fingers into a crown as it strode nonchalantly along the bustling city street. Adrianne stopped to examine what she could so clearly see, yet everyone else seemed blind to it.

The elk turned to face Adrianne. They considered each other for a long pause, gazing into each other's eyes. They were momentarily interrupted by a tourist double-decker bus. After it passed, they resumed their connection. Then the elk lifted its head as if in a nod and sauntered away. Adrianne watched as it disappeared into the crowd.

She remained on the street corner, blocking the path, and got pushed and shoved, not out of rudeness, but simply because she was in the way. Her mind was now blank. She had been considering something. Something strange that she could not remember. It was possible that the heat was affecting her. The sun beat down warmly over her face and hair. She moved away from the corner towards the shade of a storefront's awning, fumbling in her purse, searching for a piece of tissue so that she could wipe her nose and dab the perspiration from under her eyes.

Her phone buzzed.

"Hey, Helen, I'm on my way.... Oh.... Umm, yeah, no, I understand.... Yeah, that's okay. Don't worry. It's fine.... Maybe next week.... Yeah, really don't worry about it.... I'll see you later.... Yeah, bye."

Damn. It was just a lunch. An ordinary lunch. But Adrianne needed to talk. Something was happening at home. Something she felt through her skin. Something that if spoken to a trusting ear she might find was nothing but a wisp of smoke. But she needed to be assured that her imagination was working overtime before her fears gained form and weight.

Going home was not something she really wanted to do. And the streets were so full today. Vendor tables were lined up along the edges of the sidewalk with handmade crafts, T-shirts, scarves, leather holders for pocket gadgets. The table nearest to her had some jewelry that was interesting. She waited patiently while another woman examined a bracelet. The woman put it on and the shiny metal loops looked exotic and graceful on her wrist. Adrianne gently squeezed past her to pick up a necklace of polished stones that glittered over twisted bronze and copper. She held it up, decided it was too extravagant, and put it down. She looked at a few pairs of earrings, trying them against her face in the small plastic mirror hanging from the stand. None of them appeared as nice on her as they did on the table, so she put them back as well. The heat of the seller's stare told her he was about to make the hard pitch for a sale. She gave the table one final look before he could speak, then walked away.

Voices, accents, languages whose rhythms echoed places Adrianne had never seen (and maybe never would) beat past her like a marching band. The sounds were a blending stream of conversations and sighs. The faces that passed her were from all over the world. Each a different shape and color. The smell of roasting peanuts on open charcoal burners, curried meats, frying falafels, and urine from the gutters drifted through the heated summer air. Adrianne moved asynchronously in the uneven flow of people. Many in the crowd carried multiple shopping bags stamped with designer logos, walking credit card bills with grinning faces.

The open doors of the boutiques and electronic stores blasted icy wind from air conditioners set on super-high. The cold beckoned to her. She relished the cool against her skin. Through her reflection on the window of a clothing store she could see the plastic people looking at the mannequins in their styled outfits. She went inside to join them.

She roamed through the racks of shirts, skirts, dresses, and pants. The perfume of a passing salesgirl was a mixture of sea breezes and powder. She clicked her price gun on a tag.

A red and white blouse caught Adrianne's eye. She pulled it off the rack and held it up to the light. It was a flowing delicate faux silk blouse, long at the bottom with buttons at the top. She put it next to her body in front of a mirror. It was too young for her, so she replaced it on the rack without much care. She really shouldn't be here, she thought. She wasn't going to buy anything anyway. Back out to the summer streets.

The sun pierced her skin like a blade. She looked up and saw a dot of green hovering in the blue sky. It hung there for a few moments, and then it was gone. She paused to look for the dot, staring up from under scaffolding that provided cover from the heat. She leaned against the metal pole that held the wooden planks above, waving a newspaper at herself, as if the hot wind it produced could actually make her feel cooler. The headlines told of the possibility of war in some foreign land. Same old shit.

God, there is construction everywhere in this damn city. When are they gonna be done building this place?

"Hey, lady, look out!"

```
*** SYSTEM FAILURE ***

CREATING FILE: core.dmp

>>
>>
>> opendoc /r core.dmp
ERROR: CANNOT OPEN FILE

>> opendoc /d core.dmp
FILE: core.dmp 0 odus

>>
>>
>> delete core.dmp

*FILE DELETED*

>>
>> bypass error

SYSTEM ERROR BYPASSED

>> restart

BRIDGE PROCESS: **RESTARTED**
  .

  .

  .
```

"Lady, you okay?"

He was brown, skin and eyes, and covered in dust. He looked shaken, as if he'd seen the hand of death. Adrianne lay on the ground, also enshrouded in dust. He took off his yellow hard hat and cautiously touched her on the face and neck with calloused hands. Adrianne reached up to feel the wetness on her forehead. The red on her open palm sent a sourness to her stomach.

"Easy now," he said. "The paramedics will be here in a minute."

When Antoine finally came home, Adrianne knew exactly what he would say when he noticed the huge bandage on her forehead. "Why don't you watch where you're going?"

And true to form, that was exactly what he said after the prerequisite: "Are you all right?" and "Can I get you anything?"

"Yes, of course, I'm all right and no, thank you, I don't want anything. I'm fine. I have a little headache. It's not like the scaffolding actually fell on me or anything. It was just a scare. If you don't mind I would like to get some rest. It's been a hell of a day."

His tired eyes stared down at her. Maybe he wanted to hold her in his arms. But something stopped him. In the old days, he would have been all over her with caresses and kisses. There would never have been a doubt in her mind about his love.

Night was draining away and the yellow of the morning drifted through the window. It was 6:18 a.m. and her head still throbbed. It was so quiet. Barely a car horn or voice. Antoine snored in the living room. Adrianne was curled up in their bed alone. Of late, Antoine preferred the couch to being next to her. She touched his unslept side of the bed. He had taken his pillow. The place where it had been was flat and empty. The tabby jumped up on the bed and mewed, then massaged her thigh. He wanted his breakfast. Why couldn't he bother Antoine instead sometimes?

She and the cat crept quietly past the couch so as not to wake him. He woke anyway. He faced her and poked at the corners of his eyes to remove the crust there. He was embarrassed. *He should be*, Adrianne thought. A flush of heat rose to her cheeks, and she passed him to go into the kitchen to feed the one male in the house that she didn't despise at the moment.

Antoine shuffled in like an old lady in his slippers and stood next to her, still rubbing his eyes. He wore nothing but his boxers, and his hair was as spiked and spindly as a porcupine's. The smell of sleep was heavy upon him, a mixture of sweat and yesterday's cologne. He brushed past her and mumbled, "Sorry."

Adrianne nodded without looking at him. The cat was impatient and mewed in earnest.

"It's coming. It's coming. Shh!" she said to the cat. He continued to yowl in a rhythm of his own making. The scraping on the bottom of the can, the occasional sighs, the opening and closing of cabinet and fridge doors produced a song of a lonely kitchen. The cat finally calmed once Adrianne bent down to place his bowl in front of him.

Antoine ground some coffee, then set some water in the kettle to boil. Adrianne pulled open drawers, searching for aspirin, anything for her head. Then she remembered the prescription from the Emergency Room for painkillers.

"Would you call in my prescription to the pharmacy?" she asked.

"Hmm?"

"My prescription," she repeated. "Would you call it in? They might deliver it. Would you ask them to do that?"

"Yeah, sure," he said, not looking up from pouring ground coffee into his French press. The kettle steamed, then shook as it prepared itself to boil.

"So what's going on here?" Adrianne said. Venom dripped from each word.

"What?"

"You tell me 'what.'"

He shrugged.

"Look at me!"

"What?" He turned around and for a half second met her eye.

"What's going on? Why are you acting this way? Did I do something?"

"Nothing's wrong." He reached for the kettle and poured hot water into his carafe. The water turned brown. "How's your head?"

She slapped a dishcloth down on the counter and left the kitchen.

The purse she used the day before was hanging on the bedroom closet doorknob. It still had dust on it. She fished around inside, looking for her prescription slip. It lay half crumpled and a bit torn on the bottom. Unpronounceable words were scripted on the little form, signed by a doctor she barely remembered seeing.

She flattened out the slip and returned to the living room and sat on the couch surrounded by Antoine's disheveled sheets. Her arm lay on his still warm pillow. The muskiness of his sweat swirled around her. She closed her eyes and breathed.

Antoine meandered out of the kitchen carrying his coffee mug. The cat jumped up on the couch, contented and full with his breakfast. He crawled in circles on her lap several times before he found the right spot to settle down into. He purred loudly, hypnotically. She fell under his spell, stroked his soft fur, scratched him behind the ears. For a moment, she forgot the pulsing pounding in her head.

Something tapped at the window. Maybe the wind. She gazed up from petting the cat and saw a large owl sitting on the ledge. She blinked several times. It was still there, twisting its neck slightly to the right like an Egyptian hieroglyph dancer. Its white face was in the shape of a heart, with black penetrating eyes. Adrianne's body went numb, her mouth dry. She couldn't move. She could only focus on the owl. The cat moved beneath her hand. He was staring at the window, too. His tail puffed out and his heart raced against her thigh.

A jingle of keys interrupted her. Antoine sauntered out of the bedroom dressed in his business casual, ready to leave for work.

"I'm going to be working late tonight," he said, "so don't wait for me for dinner."

Adrianne could barely speak. "What?"

"I said to not wait for me for dinner tonight. What are you looking at?"

"Don't you see it?"

"See what?"

She stammered the words, feeling crazy and wanting to take them back even as she spoke them. "The bird outside the window."

"What bird?"

She turned away for only a moment. When she looked back, there was no owl, only open sky interrupted by high-rise apartment buildings like their own. The cat calmly slept on her lap.

Antoine walked up to the window. "Oh, I see..." he said.

Adrianne jumped up, tossing the cat to the floor.

"...it's only the owl statue for scaring the pigeons."

A stone sculpture of an owl sat on the ledge facing the skyline, unmoving and quite fake looking. It was doubtful if even the pigeons would be fooled by it.

"I thought I saw it move," she said. "I guess my mind is playing tricks on me."

"Maybe you should stay home today," Antoine said.

"Yeah," she said, not taking her eyes off the stone owl.

"But like I said, I'll be home late. It's a business thing. I can't get out of it."

Adrianne nodded her head and rubbed her neck.

"You okay?"

She felt herself frown. This was not the man who still cared for her. He was a guy doing the minimum to be considered polite. If she had been a stranger who slipped and fell on the street, he would have done the same. Then once he saw that she was okay, she was none of his concern.

"We should talk," she said.

"I don't have time right now."

"Then when?"

"Maybe when I get home. I gotta go. I don't wanna be late for work."

In a few steps he was at the door.

"Are you going to leave me?" Adrianne said.

The tension in his shoulders told her what she needed to know.

"I'll see you when I get home," he said as he put on his jacket and walked out the door.

He must be really distracted to put on his jacket in this heat, she thought. The *click click* of his steps echoed in the empty hallway outside the closed door. Her world spun on a wobbly axis; her stomach turned. Her head pounded. She had forgotten to give him her prescription. It was still in her pocket.

The stone owl sat cold and unmoving on its ledge. She had never noticed it before. Adrianne studied its form, its size, its color. It wasn't the owl of her vision from moments ago. It was smaller and a different shape. And how could she have seen it from where she'd been sitting on the couch? The cat had seen it, too. Hadn't he?

A blue untroubled sky filled with soft rolling clouds of puffy white hung suspended above the city. A lone airplane, the length of her pinky's nail, crept ever so slowly past. The street below was beginning its day, workers crowding it as they made their way to their jobs. From this height, it was difficult to distinguish the people, but the trees...the leaves were golden brown. It must be fall. But she could have sworn it was summer...

```
>>
>>
>> break

**. SYSTEM INTERRUPT **

>> state status

STATUS: NORMAL

>>
>> continue

BRIDGE PROCESS: CONTINUED
.

.

.
```

2.

The pills put Adrian to sleep, and he slept like the dead. When he woke up, his head still hurt. It was a dull pain with less of the pounding than before. The bandage was gone. It must have fallen off in the bed somewhere.

In the bathroom, he bent down into the sink and tossed water on his face. His jaw felt funny and his skin was rough. The place where that little hair kept appearing on his chin seemed to have spread into stubble all across his face. The mirror stared back, and he was surprised at what he saw. It was the same jaw line. The same stubble that appeared every twelve or so hours. But for a second, he didn't recognize the face. He rubbed his head and pulled out a new bandage.

Antoine was still asleep when Adrian crept into his room. The machines were all right. Beeping along quietly. His heart still pumped blood. His lungs still breathed air. Antoine seemed so peaceful when he slept. So thin. So frail. Adrian suppressed a twinge of pain and bent down to place a soft kiss on his forehead. He wouldn't wake. It took a lot more than that to wake him. He did stir, but only for a moment. Adrian slipped out as he had slipped in, being careful to pull the door quietly shut behind him.

The shower felt good. Warm water washed over his body. He gave in to his need to take care of his own business and tugged at his cock.

He thought of Antoine and released into sorrow.

The morning routine was easy now. Adrian made his own breakfast first, then Antoine's. By the time the nurse arrived, Antoine would be all set. The blender whirred his banana mush cereal. He threw in extra vitamins. It might not help, but it wouldn't hurt.

"Antoine?" Adrian softly said. He didn't stir. "Antoine?" He was taking too long to wake. Adrian shook him, a pang of terror shooting down into his groin.

"Antoine!"

His eyes snapped open. "What?"

Adrian breathed and caressed his face.

"Breakfast," in almost a whisper.

"Yeah? Oh." He weakly smiled. His teeth were gray and dark in places. His skin was tight along his cheekbones and eyes. Spots danced across a face that had once been so smooth and clear.

"Let me help you," Adrian said and easily lifted him into a sitting position. Antoine used to put up a fuss. Lately, he submitted to his situation. Their situation. Adrian placed the tray over his legs and tucked a napkin into his nightshirt. He fed him like a baby, wiping his mouth where it dripped. Antoine put up his hand to say he wanted to stop for a minute. He chewed methodically, then swallowed with an audible gulp.

"How's your head?" he asked.

"Better," Adrian said.

Adrian attempted to feed him more. Antoine stopped him by putting his hand on Adrian's wrist.

"Where are you going today?"

Adrian hesitated. It was his day off, and Antoine knew where he was going.

"To the gym."

Adrian spooned some more mush. Antoine squinted, a little burn of fire behind his glance, but took the food willingly.

As Antoine was finishing his last bite of mush, the doorbell rang. Right on time. Adrian greeted Sheila at the door like the godsend she was. Without her, Adrian couldn't survive this. She was a big, brown, no-nonsense woman. Once a week Adrian got this. Once a week to live like a normal person. Once a week without Antoine. Again the guilt. But he needed it. The counselor at the clinic said that he should get out of the house sometimes. Leave the sickness behind for a while and breathe the fresh air and do things that were just for him.

"What the hell happened to you?" Sheila asked, pointing at the bandage on his forehead.

"Oh, this." He touched his bruise. "I had a little accident yesterday."

"You okay?"

"Yeah, I'm fine. It's nothing."

Adrian returned to the bedroom to pick up the tray with the empty dishes.

"Is that Sheila?"

"Yes."

"So you're leaving soon?"

"In a few minutes."

"When will you be coming home?"

"Later this afternoon." Sheila was on the clock for a full eight hours. Antoine knew that. He asked every week anyway.

"Call me if he needs anything," Adrian said to Sheila as she walked into the bedroom.

"You know I will. Don't worry, honey. We'll be just fine."

Her toothy smile was the reassurance it was meant to be. Adrian kissed Antoine on the forehead.

"I'll be home soon."

Antoine didn't say goodbye. He barely looked at Adrian.

Cool crisp air brushed against his cheeks. The trees were losing their green and turning gold and yellow. There was a tinge of the winter cold that was to come. It was bracing. The walk to the gym always cleared his head. He stopped at the front desk and the usual guy was there with his over-whitened teeth. Adrian handed him his gym ID card to wave over the scanner to a beep. White Teeth handed the card back and said, "Have a good workout" in a syrupy, synthetic voice. He knew. Everyone knew. It was a small neighborhood.

"Thanks."

Adrian started his workout with a run on the treadmill. He selected the James Taylor playlist on his personal player and exercised to its sad, country-styled rhythms. He never told Antoine about his Taylor workouts. He would probably laugh and say, "I'm taking away your gay card." Adrian smiled to himself at the untold joke. It was a strange feeling, to smile.

He was hot and sweaty by the time he reached the weight room. "The boys" were all there. They waved hellos. Those guys seemed to live here. Muscles were flexing everywhere. The room smelled of men. Hot, sweaty men. It wasn't a pleasant smell, in some ways. In others, it was irresistible. Adrian suddenly felt the need to focus.

Hector waltzed over and slapped him on the shoulder. "Hey, Papi. How you doin'?"

"Hi, Hector," he said, his arm fully engaged in lifting a weight. He used that as an excuse to not look up.

"What happen to your head?"

"A small accident. It's nothing."

"An accident? Oh, Papi, you know you gotta be careful."

"Yeah," Adrian said, still not looking up.

"Well, we goin' to brunch in a few minits. You comin'?"

"Where?"

"The usual place. Notin' special."

"Yeah, sure. Let me shower and I'll be out."

"No problem, Papi. We wait for you."

The usual place was the brunch *spot*. Everyone from the neighborhood was there. Adrian and Antoine used to come here together back before he got sick. They would meet up with friends and laugh for hours on a Sunday mid-morning, as Adrian was about to do. The twelve of them asked for the big table in the corner. When they were seated Hector dropped himself into a chair far on the other side. Adrian was glad for that. It felt good to be out with the boys. They were buffed, beautiful men, and they knew it. The waiter flirted with them and wiggled his back feathers. They laughed at his antics. They laughed at each other. They just laughed. Especially Adrian. Once a week for this. This one time to forget about it all and laugh.

It was lunch for Adrian—he'd been up since early. For the others, it was still breakfast time. Pancakes and waffles and scrambled eggs was the going fare. Adrian liked the blueberry pancakes here, so that's what he ordered—to be one with the "fellas"—with a tall glass of orange juice.

Adrian could feel everyone being extra nice to him. He did his best to ignore it. But once in a while, the heat of someone's long stare burned the back of his neck, and he couldn't help meeting the sympathetic eyes of a friend. Adrian would turn away quickly. He didn't want sympathy. He wanted a normal time. His laugh was as loud as anyone's—maybe a bit louder.

When brunch was over, they settled up the bill and said their goodbyes. Tommy hugged him extra tight. The sound of him drawing back sniffles filled Adrian's ear. When their embrace ended, he kissed Adrian on the cheek and was all smiles.

"You be strong, 'kay," Tommy said.

Adrian watched the group file away into different directions until they were finally gone. Now it was just Adrian and Hector.

They walked up the street together, glancing in the shop windows. This was an area for tea shoppes, clothing boutiques, antique stores, and such. They stopped at a store with a display of scarves and knickknacks.

"Dey have the best candles in here," Hector said and pulled open the door. Adrian followed. Hector fussed about, sniffing at candles of all sizes. Adrian stood by a table of glass figurines. He held one of the delicate animals up to the light. It was a translucent elk with winding antlers elegantly formed high upon its tiny head. Hector returned with a candle in hand.

"Smell dis," he said shoving the candle in Adrian's face. "Isn't dat purfect?"

"It's nice," Adrian replied.

"Good, 'cus I'm getting it."

Hector collected two more candles and went to the counter to pay for them.

They left the shop and entered the not-so-busy street. A few people passed, no one interesting.

"You wanna come over my howse?" Hector asked.

"Yeah," Adrian said, "let's go."

The hallways echoed their steps as they made their way to Hector's apartment. Occasionally they passed a door where the sound of music or yelling or the roaring giddiness of children's laughter could be heard. Adrian stood behind Hector as he turned the many locks to his door. It opened to a very small place. Hector lived alone, so that was okay. He opened the window to let in the cool afternoon breeze.

"Papi, you wan anythin' to drink?"

"No, I'm good," Adrian said as he sat down on the big, black, almost-leather sofa. It made a farting sound as he sank into it. He adjusted himself to make sure that he made the sound again.

"I'll be right out," Hector said and disappeared into his bedroom.

Hector came back and sat next to Adrian with smiling eyes. He placed a box of condoms on the coffee table. Adrian unbuckled his belt and slid open his fly. His penis practically popped out. Hector touched him there, and Adrian bit at his lower lip.

"Don't worry, Papi. It's alright," Hector said in a whisper and went down on his knees in front of Adrian, stroking his cock. Adrian closed his eyes and fell into the moment. Sinking into the couch, he felt Hector's tongue on him and then the condom came slowly rolling down, then a whole mouth. Hector slurped and slurped and gently pulled. When Adrian opened his eyes, it was to stare out the window. An owl was there. Its white heart-shaped face blinked. Adrian closed his eyes again. Her long legs surrounded him. Her soft breasts brushed his chest. She opened and forced herself down on his member to grind. God, it felt so good. Adrian reached up to cup her breasts. Her nipples were hard in his palms.

"Helen..." he whispered. She moaned. He grabbed behind her to pull her ass down.

```
>>
>>
** SYSTEM INTERRUPT **

ERROR: FRAGMENTATION
```

```
ERROR: CORRECTED

BRIDGE PROCESS: **RESUMED**
```

.

.

.

A head of curls filled Adrian's hands as Hector worked his tongue all over his cock. Hector reached his hand down there. Adrian couldn't stop.

"I'm sorry...I..."

The tears came, and he released into sorrow.

Hector finished by stroking his deflating thing. It was still sensitive and moved to his touch.

"Is there something you wanna tell me, Papi?"

"Wha?" Adrian said dreamily, tears streaming down his cheeks.

"Who's Helen?" Hector looked up. Then he noticed Adrian's face and stopped smiling. "Oh, Papi. You alright?"

Adrian wiped his face and didn't answer, but eased himself up. Hector moved out of the way.

"I need to shower," Adrian said and went to the bathroom.

This would be Adrian's third shower of the day. He stepped into the stall, feeling the warmth of the flow fall over his head and shoulders. He soaped himself and pulled at his penis. He wanted to be clean. The thought of Antoine and his frail skin lying in his sickbed filled his chest. Adrian leaned on the wall as the water from his eyes mixed with the water of the shower. Hector came in.

"Papi... You okay?"

"Yeah," he lied.

He didn't turn around.

Hector undressed and slipped into the shower. He stroked Adrian and soaped him all over—first his back, then shoulders, then his butt. Hector fingered him. Adrian didn't like this part, but it was what Hector needed.

"Ay, Papi..." Hector reached around to Adrian's cock, pulled gently, entered him.

"Ay... Ay... Ay... Ay... Pa-pi... Ay..."

Adrian went away somewhere and was someone else.

Hector lifted Adrianne, she was so light. She held onto the shower rod as he pulled into her. He cupped her breasts in his hand. The water and soap made them slide. Adrian felt dizzy. He was himself again and stroked his chest. It was muscular and flat.

"Ay...   Ay...   Ay...   Ay-yay-yay...ooooohhhhh, Paaaapeeeee..."

Hector panted on Adrian's back and gently kissed him there. "Mi amore, Papi," he said and slipped out of the shower. Adrian rinsed himself as Hector left him alone in the bathroom. He found a towel and wrapped it around his waist, then sat on the toilet seat lid and bowed his head.

Adrian was fully dressed when he came out of the bathroom. Hector, still in a towel, had a beer waiting for him. Adrian took a few sips, tasted the light bitterness, then put the bottle down.

"Will I see you again next week?" Hector asked.

"Maybe." Adrian didn't know what else to say.

"It's alright, Papi. I understand.... How is Antoiny?"

Adrian hated that he used his name. And no one called him "Antoiny."

"He's okay." Adrian corrected himself, "He's the same."

"Oh."

"I need to go home now. The nurse will be leaving soon."

Hector touched his face and said, "Mi amore, Papi. It's gonna be alright."

Adrian hated him for that.

He grabbed his jacket from the hook behind the door and left.

Home was a place of sorrow. A place of love. It was difficult to reconcile the two. All the silence of the world was there. It was as if they lived in a special bubble separate from all that existed in time and space. Adrian didn't want to live in that bubble. But it was where Antoine lay, so it was where he must go.

"Hey, baby," Sheila said. "You enjoy your time off?"

Adrian mumbled. Then smiled, remembering that he shouldn't be rude.

"It was okay."

Sheila had been cooking. The sweet smell of her curried meat scented the air. This was not a required duty, but she did it anyway. At first, Adrian thought she did it because she wanted bigger tips. Then he realized the true reason was much simpler, purer: she liked them.

"Here, baby, let me take your things," she said, as she carried away his jacket and gym bag. Her banter was momentarily muffled by the closet as she leaned in. It didn't matter. The rhythm of her speech was what Adrian really listened to. It calmed him. There was a lightness to Sheila that defied her heavy bulk. Adrian wished he could be like her. He didn't think he could ever be that sane. The walk back home had not been easy. He felt sick with every step. It was like he was walking in a dark misty cloud. Sheila's friendly voice was a welcome wash of clear water.

"I left something on the stove for you. You can warm it up for dinner."

"Thanks."

"You better eat it up, baby. A grown man like you shouldn't be so damn skinny." She laughed. He couldn't help but laugh a little, too.

"Is he awake?"

"Yeah, he's awake. We were just playing cards when you came in."

Antoine didn't look up when Adrian entered the room. Long plastic lines of fluids connected to drip tubes that connected to bags of liquid that connected to machines. The complex spider's web surrounded Antoine, delivering to his frail, failing body life-sustaining medicines. Antoine and the machines were becoming one. They were lucky to be able to afford all this. Since the disease had spread, such equipment was scarce and expensive.

There was a deck of cards in Antoine's hands. He used to be remarkably nimble at shuffling. He'd flip cards like acrobats, then split them into piles of two, fan them out, and shove them back together as if forming a loaf of bread. Now he slowly slid them around on his tray, lifting a corner of one to expose its face, then slid them around some more.

"Well, that's it for me," Sheila said at the doorframe. "I'll see you two next week." She pursed her lips. "And don't play cards with that sucker. He cheats."

Antoine simpered while still concentrating on the cards. "I'm not the cheater around here."

Cold blood rushed to Adrian's head.

"Well, see you guys next week."

"I'll see you out," Adrian said, leaving the room as fast as he could.

He walked Sheila to the door, accepting her goodbye hug like the friend she was.

"You okay?" she said.

"Yeah, I'm fine. Just a little tired."

"Well, if you need anything you have my number."

"Yes, thanks Sheila. Have a good week."

"Yes, you too. Remember to take it one day at a time."

When she was gone, all the safety went with her. He faced the bedroom like a Neanderthal standing before the opening of a dark cave. Who knew what danger lurked within? Adrian opened the door to find Antoine staring into space.

"So how is he?" Antoine asked.

"Who?" Adrian replied.

"You know who, *Papi*."

Adrian sat down. There was no need to ask how he'd found out. It was a small neighborhood. Heifers talk. Antoine was as capable of getting phone calls as he ever was.

"You know that it doesn't mean anything."

Antoine looked down at his hands.

"Yeah, I know."

"...I'm sorry."

"Don't be. We agreed you could see other people... I just wish it wasn't him."

The machines that chirped in time to Antoine's heart barely registered a flutter. If they had been attached to Adrian, they would sound like a conga band.

"It's just a thing. I don't care about him."

"Does *he* know that?" Antoine met Adrian's eyes. "He's only waiting for me to die so he can finally have you."

"Don't say that!"

19

The air sucked out of Adrian's lungs. All sound disappeared. The room floated around and around, spinning and spinning.

```
** CORE INTERRUPT **

DETECTED MAJOR FAULT @ SECTOR: 10110001
SYSTEM RE-ROUTE IN PROGRESS
    .

    .

    .
```

"Don't ever say that!"

"It's true," Antoinette said. "You know it's true. Promise me that you won't choose her after I'm gone. Anyone but her."

"I don't want to talk about this."

"Well, I do! Promise me you won't choose her. Helen is trouble, Adrianne. She might be good for an afternoon fuck, but that's it."

"I don't want to talk about this."

"You're going to have to deal with what's going to happen after I'm gone sooner or later."

Adrianne closed her eyes tight. "I don't want to talk about this," she repeated.

"Adrianne," Antoinette said. "Adrianne!"

Adrianne stood up to leave.

"All right, all right, don't go. Just sit down."

Antoinette began to organize cards in front of her, forming lines as if preparing to play solitaire. The sounds of ruffling cards and beeping machines filled the void. Adrianne was absorbed in the movements of her hands. They were jittery, long and thin. Antoinette could still write and use the computer, but after a while she became so tired. Her body couldn't keep up with her mind. It frustrated her. Adrianne would do anything to have Antoinette back the way she had been.

"I don't want you talking about dying anymore."

Antoinette raised a corner of her mouth in an anemic grin and said, "Okay."

Antoinette began coughing. She raised herself slightly and bent over to hack so deeply that phlegm flew out. Adrianne wiped her mouth with a tissue.

They were waiting by a river for the boat that would come all too soon. When it did, they both knew that Antoinette would be a passenger. She was leaving, and Adrianne couldn't stop her. She desperately wanted Antoinette to get up from her bed and walk. They could go anywhere she wanted. She'd take her to the ends of the world, if only she didn't get on that boat.

"I don't want you to leave me," Adrianne said, her lungs like canisters of warm jelly. The water of sorrow ran like a river down the curve of Adrianne's cheek. She wiped it away, but more freely came.

"Come here, baby," Antoinette said.

Adrianne carefully snaked through the tubes and wrapped her arms around Antoinette. Antoinette was a tiny bird. So light and delicate like lace. Her ricey hair was balding in spots. It was once so full and beautiful, a bounty of curls and waves. Adrianne kissed her scalp and folded her into her chest.

"You're my baby always," she said. "And I'm your girl 'til the day I die."

```
>>
>>
** RESET **
.
.
.
```

3.

In the stillness and the shadows, among the crumpled clothes scattered about the floor and the dust bunnies that roamed the bedroom like tumbleweeds in a ghost town, lay Adrianne. The curtains were drawn. Lines of light slipped through the edges and along the seams. They hadn't been open for...since... It had been a while. It was day outside. There was life out there. And Adrianne wanted no part of it. They called it heartache because that was what it was, the heart ached and moaned for the hurt. An agonizing numbness wrapped around her chest like a vise. Antoinette was gone. And there was nothing that was gonna bring her back.

The doorbell rang. Adrianne kept her eyes shut.

A pounding on the door.

"I know you're in there! Open up, honey, it's me!" Helen shouted.

Leave me alone. God, just leave me alone.

Keys tinkled in the lock. The damn bitch still had the set that Adrianne had given to her long ago for emergencies. Adrianne sank deeper into the bed and twisted in the sheets. Helen entered, stepping through the apartment. Kitchen plates clicked, water ran over days of unwashed dishes, chairs scraped the floor. Magazine pages flipped in the living room, papers were rifled through, the letters and bills that had been left scattered on the coffee table were shuffled into stacks. Then slowly the bedroom door opened.

"Adrianne?" she whispered.

Silence.

"Adrianne, are you in here?"

"Please leave me alone," Adrianne said. Her throat was dry and hoarse from disuse. Words were useless. Only in her dreams did she speak or sing or dance.

Helen sat down at the edge of the bed. Just let me sleep, Adrianne thought, I'm warm under these sheets. Cocooned from everything. It was easier to live in dreams than to feel the harshness of the air and the light and the sounds. Only sleep was a solace for sorrow.

"Honey...look at you...." Helen paced her words. This was a delicate operation.

"Please, go away."

"I'm your friend. I can't leave you like this.... I know it hurts, but it's been months...."

"Leave me alone!" Adrianne screamed. Her words spewed forth like hot liquid.

"I will not leave you alone!"

Adrianne could feel Helen's hand searching through the sheets to find her. It landed on her arm.

"Antoinette would not want this for you. It's been too long. Today you're getting cleaned up and going out into the sun. We are going outside together and having a nice meal somewhere like normal people." She flung back the sheets, exposing Adrianne to the cold.

The shower stall was a clear glass-enclosed closet. Steam was her only curtain. Water spread over her like a cleansing rain. Its warmth stimulated her limbs and soaked her skin. Shampoo with the scent of lilac splashed into her eyes and stung. She scrubbed and scrubbed, then shaved. Dry flaky skin turned into a darkened flow where it streamed toward the drain and gathered with the foamy remains of soap. Adrianne was angry with Helen for invading her space, and she loved her for it. Her presence outside the bathroom door made Adrianne feel responsible, somehow. Not better, just more responsible. She had to clean up; someone was here. She had to eat; someone was watching. She had to shave her armpits; someone could smell.

Adrianne turned off the water and stood enshrouded in a steam so thick she could hardly breathe. Nothing held her, only the moist air. She was lost in time, surrounded by a warm humidity, while thoughts of Antoinette, buried and decomposing in the soil, whirled in her mind. She hugged herself and rocked as if in prayer, then leaned against the wet tile, moaning softly to herself.

"Hey, you all right in there?" Helen shouted from the other side of the door.

"I'm fine," Adrianne said too quickly, with a flash of fear that Helen might come inside.

"You're so quiet.... Okay, take your time. When you come out, I have a surprise for you."

Adrianne sat on the toilet and let the warm pee stream out of her. Then she stood and stared, mesmerized by her yellow creation. She flushed. Her moist hand wiped the fogged mirror of the medicine cabinet. Facing back was her and not her. She was somebody else. Someone she didn't recognize. Someone she didn't want to recognize.

"Sweetie?" The door quietly opened and Helen's head came into view. "Oh, honey..." she said as she let herself in. She put her arms around Adrianne's shoulders, then brushed back her wet hair.

"I'm getting you out of this morbid place. At least for one afternoon you're going to forget all this."

"But I don't want to forget."

"You can't live like this." They stared at each other in the mirror. Adrianne nodded.

"Come on and get dressed." Helen led her back to the bed to sit while she rummaged through the closet. In her right mind she would have told Helen to get the hell out of there. Nobody touched her clothes. Or told her how to dress. But that was before. The hangers scraping against the wooden closet pole sounded like birds screeching. At last Helen emerged with her silk red blouse and a dark blue pair of pants. She held the outfit up proudly. "I always liked you in this shirt, and these will look good with it, don't you think?"

Adrianne took the clothes and began putting them on without questioning Helen's taste.

"I've got a surprise for you," Helen said. "I scored two tickets to this afternoon's games, and you and I are going!"

Adrianne made a questioning face.

"It will be fun! There might even be some celebrities in the audience."

Adrianne didn't know what the hell she was talking about. She had never known Helen to have an interest in sports. Adrianne sighed. The small breath released some of her melancholy.

"But first, there is lunch. I know this cute little place downtown where we can sit outside and eat and watch the people go by."

The smells of the city were strange—new—different. The faintest hint of fresh dung lingered from somewhere. Adrianne remembered that smell from when she was a kid and the neighbors spread manure on their vegetable garden. It was a sweet, stinky smell she found secretly pleasant. Maybe there was a horse-drawn carriage or a police horse nearby? But they were a bit far from the park where such things could be found. Her mind drifted as she sat across from Helen in an open-air cafe on the sidewalk, corralled by large potted plants and velvet ropes outside a restaurant with dining tables and flowers and menus and customers who ate and laughed and drank and smoked and were as carefree as she felt careworn.

"What are you having?" asked Helen.

"What?" said Adrianne.

"What are you going to order?"

The menu lay in front of her, ignored.

"I'll have whatever you're having," Adrianne said.

"Come now, don't be so boring. Pick something for yourself. How about the soup?"

"Sure, the soup will be fine."

She went back to searching the street for the source of the mysterious scent. Something rustled in the bushes across the street. She squinted into the leaves to see what was there. A pigeon? A sparrow? A rat? Helen was speaking. Adrianne heard the words but found herself mesmerized by a bird flying above. It circled around and around, dipping and coasting, disappearing behind the top of the building across the street, then reappearing to turn in a large O again. She had seen such strange things of late. Things she could hardly grasp and hold onto as real.

"Adrianne?"

"Hmm."

"You okay, hon?"

"I'm fine."

The soup arrived. She tasted it. It was warm and needed salt.

"How is the soup?"

"It's good."

"That's what you needed, something warm in your stomach," Helen said.

From the corner of Adrianne's eye, movement. The creature in the bush rustled the leaves. Then a singular gust of wind from high above. The bird—a hawk? an owl?—graceful wings outstretched. Swooped down. Grabbed the mysterious thing out of the bush. A squeal? A screech? A scream? Then they were gone.

"Did you see that?"

"See what?"

"That...over there."

Helen glanced over. "What?"

"Never mind," Adrianne said.

"Are you sure you're okay?"

"Yes, I'm fine." Adrianne forced a smile.

"We should hurry. The ride up to the stadium can be a bitch, but if we leave right after lunch, we should be there in time." Helen said, touching Adrianne's hand.

The stadium's archways were tall enough to accommodate giants. They curved high above her head, creating a sense of awe that was surely the designer's intent. Adrianne felt small against them, diminutive. She looked up and spun in place for a single turn as she took it all in. Her head continued to spin even after she stopped moving. Dizzy, out-of-place, insignificant. Helen grabbed her hand and pulled her into line, bouncing with tickets in hand as giddy as a child about to receive forbidden candy. She reached around and half-hugged Adrianne, rubbing her back.

After a few moments of this, Adrianne took hold of Helen's hand as if in affection, but really to still its movements.

They stood in the line for those who already had tickets, and still it was very long. There were a surprising number of women among the attendees. Maybe close to half of those waiting were casually dressed females, looking as if ready to go to the market, in mostly blue denim and T-shirts with cheery slogans spread across their chests. A few sported team colors. Some of the more flamboyant ones painted wide swatches of blue, red, and white makeup across their gleeful faces.

All was orderly for those long moments spent waiting. Then the crowd shifted position like a formless sea and parted. The crush of it pushed Adrianne aside, then moved her back. The swell eventually passed like a shifting tide. She searched for the cause and found it in a woman dressed in perfect white—a white linen summer dress, white sandals , and a white scarf wrapped around her head. A little man walked before her, easing people out of the way. She glided like a white shadow, her back straight and proud, and entered an archway that seemed reserved for her. Her little guardian minded her back as she entered.

Adrianne and Helen sat in seats only twenty rows from the oval space below. Thick glass separated the audience from the field and circled the stadium. Banners blaring team names fluttered in the wind in bold reds and blues and stripes of black bordered on white. The Ravens. The Tridents. The Vulcans.

On each side of the arena, jumbo screens displayed animated fireworks between the scrolling names of the players in the games. Booming through the loudspeakers, a squeaky, high-pitched voice sang over a raunchy dance beat. Then the music changed to a bombastic marching tune, and the doors on the sides of the field opened and a pair of horses ran free. Some cheered within the shuffles and murmurs and loud conversations of those still searching for their seats.

"Wait here, I'm going to get us some popcorn," Helen said and left Adrianne alone to wonder what was in store for her this afternoon.

The sounds of the horses' hooves jerked at her heart as they galloped wild with tremendous speed and power. The vibrations shook the glass walls. The scene was breathtaking. What was unclear, though, was what the horses were doing here. For that matter, what she was doing here? This was hardly her idea of fun. And why were so many women at this sporting event? She counted them, mentally sizing them up. How many were in need of cheer like her? How many were here to forget? Helen meant well, Adrianne thought as she watched the show, but she wanted to leave.

If Antoinette were here, they would have sneaked out together by now. They would have ended up at some café, drinking chai lattes, laughing while they thought up excuses for why they had left. That was the way she was. Antoinette would never have stayed somewhere she didn't want to be. She always said that Adrianne was too soft and should assert herself more. Tears rolled down Adrianne's cheeks before she could wipe them away.

Men in orange jumpsuits drove onto the field in golf carts, rounding the horses back into the doors from where they came. Helen returned with a large tub of popcorn and maneuvered inelegantly through seats partially filled with other spectators. She plopped herself down next to Adrianne, shoving the tub into Adrianne's arms. Adrianne returned it with a wave that said she didn't want any.

"I didn't let them put too much butter on it," Helen said and munched happily on a couple of kernels.

"No thanks," Adrianne said.

A display of women dressed in white, taking their seats in a skybox, came onto the giant screens. Adrianne could almost make out their tiny white shapes, moving in the distance.

"Who are they?" Adrianne asked.

"Them?" Helen said. "They help officiate. You'll see."

All four jumbo screens now showed the oversized face of a smiling, squinty-eyed man with a lipless grin. He waved energetically to a barely acknowledging crowd.

"His majesty the mayor has gotten off his high horse and is here today," Helen said, "God, I can't stand that guy. He'll never get my vote again."

"Helen," Adrianne said, "I think I want to go home."

"What? We just got here," Helen said, dipping into the popcorn.

"Yeah, but…"

"Hey, they're about to start."

A side door opened and a sizable elk trotted onto the field of artificial green. Its tall head of antlers spread wide and pointed in all directions. It pranced about, clearly stunned. Adrianne had a nasty, sinking feeling in the pit of her stomach. It soured still more when another door opened. Something from the darkness growled angrily, then snarled. All went quiet. The elk stood stock-still. A large cat sprang out, maybe a mountain lion. It eyed the elk and ducked low, slowed its motion to small graceful steps. Adrianne wanted to yell to the elk to run. Instead she remained frozen in her seat. Her mouth went dry and her heart pounded. With incredible speed and to the cheers of the enthusiastic crowd, the cat pounced. The elk galloped, but the lion was too quick. It pulled down the elk with its mighty paws. The audience jumped to its feet and applauded wildly.

Adrianne screamed.

>>

>>

** BREAK **

```
1011000110110001101100011011000110l
1000110110001101100011011000110l100
0110110001101100011011000l101100011
0110001101100011011000110l1000l1011
0001101100011011000110l100011011000
1101100011011000110110001l011000110
1100011011000110l1000110l1000110110
001101100011011000110l1000110110001
1011000110110001101100011011000110l
1000110110001101100011011000110l100
0110110001101100011011000l101100011
0110001101100011011000110l100011011
```

```
0001101100011011000110110001101100 0
1101100011011000110110001101100011 0
1100011011000110110001101100011011 0
0011011000110110001101100011011000 1
```

\>\>

.

.

.

Adrianne's brown skin contrasted with the white linen of her chemise and the matching veil draped about her head that tied snugly under her chin. She had a perfect view of the stadium from the luxury box. Two large flat-screened televisions displayed up-close images of the carnage below. Several other women dressed in white sat in rows around her as if in a small movie theater. They had been lightly applauding at the image of the bloodied carcass of an elk, but all stopped to stare at Adrianne.

"Come on, Adrianne, it wasn't *that* bad," Helen said with popcorn in her mouth. "You better calm down. Mother is watching." And indeed she was. A stern older woman several seats back—her jaws set so tight that they protruded through her cheeks—was staring down.

"She hasn't been feeling well," Helen said to the others. The ladies nodded and returned to their murmuring.

"Maybe it wasn't such a good idea for me to come out today," Adrianne said as she wiped her moistened eyes. She put her hands in the inner pockets of her stola. A little man descended the stairs and presented a tray of Champagne glasses. She refused. Another server offered her a tray of finger sandwiches. She waved him away, and he stepped back without hesitation.

"I want to go home," Adrianne said.

"But it's just started. At least wait until halftime...."

"No, I think I should go home now."

"Are you sure?"

"Yes." Adrianne held back a sniffle.

"Okay, well, let's go home then."

"No, you stay and enjoy the rest of this. Thomas will see me home."

Thomas escorted her out of the stadium. He was a muscular man and would protect Adrianne with his life. He would never attempt to touch her, though. He was of the kind that loved other men.

Thomas commandeered a cab. A man in a business suit wanted it (and deserved it because he had actually been there first). He was about to argue with Thomas when Adrianne appeared. Her white robes hemmed in delicate purple flowed in the afternoon breeze like a sail. Business Suit backed away as Thomas held open the door for her.

The yellow cab smelled of stale cigarettes and sweat. Adrianne pressed the button to open the window. Thomas gave the cabbie directions, and they were off. During the ride she concentrated on the speeding road, her mind adrift in her sorrow. Thomas touched her hand. She turned to face him, and a drop escaped her eye. She folded into his chest. He held her there. No words. Just sorrow.

"I take it you didn't like the games."

Adrianne laughed through her sniffles.

"No, I didn't," she said.

"People expect you to like it."

"I know… I can do only what I can do… I think Mother is mad at me."

"You probably have some explaining to do tonight."

"Great."

Adrianne sat up. She pulled back her veil and took off her vitta, the headband that bound her hair together, and released her dreadlocks. She shook them loose, then finger-styled them to drape over her shoulders. The cab driver shot a dirty look at her through his rear-view mirror. Women of Adrianne's generation were demanding more freedom in the way they presented themselves, and some were openly showing their hair. Not everyone was comfortable with that. She leered at him through the mirror, daring him to challenge her. He returned his attention to the road. Adrianne sat back and closed her eyes.

Antoine.

She believed they had a connection that spread over space and time. No matter the distance, she thought that somehow, they would always find each other. Then, just like that, the dream was over. There was a barrier they could not cross, a place he could go where she could not follow. He was gone.

The cab pulled up to the entrance of the Cloisters and Thomas helped her out.

4.

From the time she was a little girl, Adrianne wore white. White veils, white dresses, white panties and then white bras. Whiteness was purity. Whiteness was good. Whiteness was strength. It was her shield and armor. Her brown skin covered always in white. It granted her access to all places unhindered. Even when she didn't realize it, there was always someone moving out of her way, opening a door, giving up a seat. This privilege—this honor—was given to her in exchange for a promise. A promise that she would inwardly be as innocent and pure as she appeared. A promise to remain a woman-child. A promise she had kept for fifteen years, half of her appointed period of time. But Adrianne had a secret.

The soft sounds of her sandals scraping the stone-tiled floor resounded beneath the high ceilings of the Cloisters' inner hall. She was alone. Thomas had gone to his room in the lower levels. Everyone else was at the games. Adrianne had the place to herself. It was a monastic hall filled with centuries-old art collected by diligent and discerning hands. Her favorite room was the one with the tapestries. A room with ceiling-high, hand-embroidered wall hangings that depicted an elk hunt. Each panel showed a different stage of the game played by noblemen of old, in search of the mystical creature who seemed to elude them at every turn. Adrianne had been told that these images held a metaphor for virginity, that the elusive elk was a symbol of the strength to withstand the temptation of copulation. It always seemed like such a thin explanation. Every time Adrianne looked upon these beautiful tapestries she thought of sacrifice and marriage.

She entered the next room. Before her the marble statue of Vesta, the veiled virgin goddess herself, looked down with maternal eyes. Within her hand was carved an oil lamp burning stone flames, and etched at her feet were stalks of wheat and barley. The image overshadowed everything. Its gaze went into far-off

33

places. The statue had been brought here from a garden in lands overseas. It was said that it had once been painted—sienna, burnt umber, olive, ochre. Its alabaster appearance was all that was left after years of exposure to the elements.

She saw this statue on the first day she arrived in these halls. It was so long ago and her memories were hazy, as if it had all happened to someone else and not her. But that night, when she was still a child and the cold pricked her skin with needles, Adrianne and her mother came here.

They rode up on the train. It was late. The only other passengers in the car were asleep with their eyes open. Purple bruises marked her mother's chin and around her left eye. She held Adrianne close as they drifted between sleep and wakefulness to the hum of the engine and the occasional rumble and scraping of metal on metal over the tracks. They passed many stations. The doors opened and closed, opened and closed. Finally they reached the end of that part of their journey, and her mother ushered Adrianne to her feet and out into a desolate subway station, a labyrinth of hallways and stairs and corners that smelled of pee.

Their heels clicked and echoed in the silence. They came to an elevator so old Adrianne was afraid to go inside. When she hesitated her mother pulled her along as she was not playing any games that night. Up and up and up, then out onto the street above. Ahead of them was an entrance to a dark place full of trees and a sign with arrows. Adrianne could read the letters, but not the words. Then, when she had no idea where she was, it had seemed the scariest of all medieval forests. A place where goblins and trolls and duppies lived. The hoot of an owl. The cry of a wolf. The growl of a cougar. She heard them all in her imagination. But it was just a garden path leading to the Vestals' hall.

Her mother's desperate pull dragged her through the park until they came to the Cloisters. Her mother pounded on the door. Everyone was asleep because of the hour. But that did not deter her. Purple bruises gave her strength. Purple bruises made her determined. She pounded on the door until it was finally opened. A woman in white greeted them and let them inside. There was a stillness in the hall. A calm. A silence. Only the crackle of the burning wood. That's when Adrianne saw Vesta for the first time. The perfect alabaster marble statue gleamed in the light of a hearth, a slight smile on her face.

She heard her mother speak in hurried tones. Words, words, and more words. What was said made no sense. Leaving... Take her.... She's a good girl.... She's yours now.... Keep her.... Raise her.... I can't take her with me. Not one more day. Not one more hour. Not one more slap. Not one more kick.... I'm not coming back.

Her mother placed Adrianne's hand into the hand of the woman in white. Then one last hard look. Was there sorrow? A whimper. A cry. A wail. Who made those sounds?

"Hey," Thomas said. "You okay?"

His sudden appearance jolted her out of her dream.

"I'm okay. Just thinking about the past."

Thomas held her close. This was not allowed, especially while she was still in her robes. But this was Thomas. An exception for him could always be made. Within their embrace she heard him choking back tears. Then he pulled back and kissed Adrianne on the cheek.

"You be strong," he said.

She felt a twinge of guilt. For a moment she had actually forgotten her recent loss. For the first time in a long while, her mind was on someone other than the person Thomas assumed she was thinking of.

She went to her cell on the upper floors—a small cubical area in one large shared room for all the girls. She curled up in bed, and drowned in her sheets. Sleep did not come easily. She tossed and turned until she found herself lying in bed staring at the high ceiling, listening to the silence until the sun went down and the room went dark, then the lights turned on. The silence was broken by the movement of careful feet as the others returned home from the games.

There were twelve Sisters. Four were the Sisters who were best friends (who now attended the flames). Two were Sisters who were more than that. One was the-girl-with-the-curly-red-hair-that-was-slowly-turning-auburn. One was Stephanie the brave.

One was Helen. One was the-girl-with-the-gray-eyes-who-didn't-speak-too-much. One was the Mother. The last was Adrianne.

In the night, the wind howled. Adrianne listened to the rain come down. It calmed quickly. It was if someone had opened a faucet, then shut it again. She fell asleep and wrestled in her dreams. In her sleep she was herself, but not herself. She went to the in-between space, neither here nor there, moving in and out of her body with ease, being herself, then staring at herself. It felt real. So fluid and natural, she was herself—just different.

Adrianne woke the next morning at the pre-dawn hour. In the cool of the morning she realized how odd her night had been. What felt natural in her dreams was now strange. Adrianne was herself and no one else. Reality was reality. And reality didn't change.

Today it would be her and Helen and the-girl-with-the-gray-eyes-who-didn't-talk-too-much and Stephanie tending the fire in Memorial Park. They ate a light breakfast, a little fruit, tea with no sweetener, and a piece of bread.

"Come on, girls, let's get this one started," Stephanie said, and the four stood up, scraping their chairs across the hard stone floors.

Adrianne hurried to the baths for her ritual cleansing. She put on her best starched white frock, bundled up her locs into the six traditional braids, and tied her hair up with a clean vitta, completing her look with a veil with a delicate purple-threaded hem. It draped loosely over her head. On the days they tended the fire they were expected to be formal and proper. One never knew who might make an appearance. Dignitaries. Film celebrities. Mourning mothers.

The wind was bracing as it came over the water. The long stone paths along the river's edge were wet from the night's rain. The four of them walked together in the customary two-by-two square. They had lobbied hard for the privilege to walk in public without an escort.

Through the park to the elevator, down into the subway, then onto the train. Adrianne always thought of her mother when she stood among the sleepy passengers on their way to work. Those not asleep moved out of their way and offered them seats. Only two girls accepted, Stephanie and Helen. Adrianne and the-girl-who-didn't-talk-too-much stood nearby holding the poles like everyone else. A wide bubble of emptiness surrounded them in the otherwise crowded car. Adrianne loved this time of the day when she could make believe she was like normal people.

An early morning mist lay over Memorial Park, the center of the city, another world, almost another place in time. And so quiet. The gentle crush of grass under sandaled feet, the swish of dew across the hems of dresses, the flap of wings overhead as a large bird flew into the trees and disappeared from view were sounds that scarcely disturbed the silence. With pathways and walkover bridges spanning slim, slinking creeks and cascading river falls, this place of green was designed to be more like a forest than an urban manicured garden.

In the old days, a small town had been located here. The city forced the residents out when it decided that the public needed a place where every citizen could sit on a spot of grass or under a tree. The park became also the place for the essential ritual of which Adrianne was a part, the keeping of the eternal flame. In the center of the park, encircled by a colonnade of Corinthian columns, stood a marble structure open to the elements with the cauldron of Vesta at its center.

The previous shift of sisters bowed gracefully to them. They looked so tired. Adrianne said hello, but none of them seemed interested in reciprocating. The rain and wind from the night before must have made their time tending the flame difficult. They quickly left, their white cloaks waving in the wind.

"What's wrong with them?" Helen asked.

"Who knows?" Stephanie said.

The Sisters began their cleaning duties. If an occasional piece of cinder, a leaf, or an acorn had fallen inside, these had to be swept away in keeping with their mandate that they maintain the area spotless. Dirt could be seen on the Sisters only while they tended the flame. The structure held only two small rooms off to the side and out of sight, a bathroom and a closet where bundles of kindling were kept. Adrianne went inside and picked up an armful of wood. She lightly tossed some of the branches onto the flame while Stephanie sprinkled on blessed water.

"Adrianne, how about after our shift we hit Twenty-five?" Helen said to Adrianne.

"Shh," Stephanie said.

Helen gave Stephanie a dirty look and quieted. She waited until the others had turned away and whispered to Adrianne, "Well, how about it?"

Vestal Vestments—V-squared, or Twenty-five—was a clothing boutique specializing in fashions for ladies of the Order. A maturing society made the veil less and less important. Soon, even the long dresses would not be worn. It was becoming acceptable to wear jeans and a T-shirt. They could appear in public like ordinary young women, as long as they dressed only in white. The younger Vestals only wore formal wear in public on special occasions or when performing their ritual duties.

"God, Helen, we were just there."

"Oh, come on, pleeeese," she sang. "It will be fun."

"Sure, fine. Whatever. After lunch."

Helen smiled with her eyes and returned to sweeping nonexistent dirt from the marble floor.

People came here for many reasons. They had lost a loved one or had some misfortune in their personal lives. They were thankful for some blessing, like the birth of a child. Or they were tourists who wanted to take pictures for the folks back home. It was customary to find a small stick in the park and attempt to hand it to one of the sisters to burn in the cauldron. It was almost a game. The sisters would pretend they didn't notice anyone. Then—when they felt like it—one of them would choose a random person from the many standing on the grass outside the structure and take his or her stick. They were often so grateful. A woman quietly waving caught Adrianne's notice. She was not very old, but her eyes were lined and red.

"In memory of my son," she said. "He died last week in the war." Adrianne bowed and approached to receive her stick, but the woman held onto it a moment longer than was necessary. They played a minor tug-of-war with it.

"Could you tell me that his death was worth it?" she asked.

People looked to her with questions like this all the time. It made Adrianne uncomfortable. She didn't know the answers, just what she was told to say.

"Your son's sacrifice was for a grateful nation." It wasn't enough. It was never enough. The eyes of the woman remained the same, maybe grew a bit darker. No comfort gained from this ritual. No solace. Adrianne climbed the marble stairs and tossed the stick in with the other faggots into the cauldron. The flames ate it hungrily.

Beyond the rows of columns, Thomas and the other guards stood. He took this opportunity to approach Adrianne and whisper in her ear. Their eyes met for a moment, then she retreated back into the building. She went inside to the bathroom. The marble walls echoed her every move. Her head felt hot, so she splashed some water on her face and dried it clumsily with a towel.

When she came back out with a bundle of sticks in her arms, Helen asked, "Hey, are you okay?"

"Yes, I'm fine," she said. "Look, Helen, I'm going to have to postpone our shopping trip this afternoon. There's something that I have to do."

Helen's eyes narrowed. "Are you sure you're okay?"

"Yes. Don't worry. Everything is fine."

Adrianne followed Thomas to a part of the city forbidden to her. They passed the tall glass and steel skyscrapers, then the area of small red brick townhouses in the lower edge of the city near the river. Thomas covered her white stola with his overcoat. Sparkling white under leather. No one should see a woman of the cloth step into such unseemly quarters. They went through back alleys where things scurried away. The sour stench of urine wafted in the air. They neared the old harbor where the great ships used to dock, an abandoned place where she had been before. Thomas helped her maneuver over rickety wooden pathways, split rotten by water and time, into a warehouse of crates and the squeaks of rats, to Room 177. Adrianne swallowed, turned the knob, and entered.

Clean and fragrant with perfume. A room familiar. A bedroom. A place she had once shared. Lit with candles. This was their place. Their secret place.

Then he entered. He wore a military uniform. Sharp. Beautiful. Healthy. Smiling. Alive! Antoine took off his beret and walked up to her and held her close. He smelled like cooled-off heat, like sweat dissipating. His bulk surrounded her. She swung in his arms, helpless with shock.

"Antoine?" Words clogged in her throat. "Thomas told me... I didn't believe... I thought you were dead."

"Dead? Why would you think I was dead? I was only gone for a few months for training." She touched his face to feel the breath from his nose and mouth on her fingers. She drank in his warmth.

"But..."

Spinning. Turning. Slipping. Sliding. This was the truth. This was a lie. This was the truth. A lie. This was real. But...it couldn't be. She remembered him. Another time. Another place. Sick and dying. Then healthy and leaving her.

```
>>
>>  .
```

```
1011000110110001101100011011000110101100011011000110110001101101
>>
```

"Shh, you silly woman. I'm fine."

"Something is wrong...."

"Nothing is wrong," Antoine said. "Not with us. Everything is as it should be."

"Everything..." Adrianne touched the nape of his neck, caressed his ear, whispered tender words too deep to recall. She kissed him on the tip of his chin. Smoothed his eyebrows. Touched the back of his head and the softness of his hair. She was his. He was hers. They were one. "Everything..."

"We don't have much time before I have to be back. The war is not going well," he said.

"The war..." she said. So far away. Meaningless to her just hours before. Now it was everything.

"I think they will be shipping me out soon."

"Then let's make the most of the time we have," she replied.

They sat on the bed together. He kissed her deeply. She tasted the sweet saltiness of him. The slip and moistness of his tongue in her mouth. The soft juiciness of his lips. She undid her robe and removed her shirt. She moved his hand to a place no one else had gone to before. A promise broken—for him. For Antoine. She opened and received all he had to give.

```
>>
>>
** BREAK **
```

```
1011000110110001101100011011000110110001101
```

.

.

.

5.

The owl, sensing the cool of the evening, opened its eyes. It turned its head to see in all directions. It was hungry. There—hiding among the trees—now in the bushes—something scurried. The something knew it was being watched. The owl waited for the slightest lapse in judgment.... Wings expanded. Wide. Wider. Fly. Fast. Faster. Talons extended, down through the air. Silent death. It pounced to take its prey squeaking into the trees. The owl snapped the thing's neck to stop its scream, then devoured it.

In the sanctuary surrounded by manicured forest, they kept the holy silence. Unnecessary noise was frowned upon. The Sisters walked close to the walls like mice and bowed their heads in greeting instead of saying hello. Their steps were slow and careful lest they make a sound. A tug on a sleeve to get the attention of another. A whisper instead of a spoken word. They lived separate from everyone in these old ways taken from the old country, just like this building, brick by brick, stone by stone, statue by statue, painting by painting. Traditions left unchanged and unquestioned and so ancient that no one remembered when they started or why. Outside, times might be changing. But behind these walls, nothing did.

Sister Adrianne posed near the inner courtyard where a tabby cat lived to enjoy watching him roam among the wild flowers and drink from the stone fountain. Adrianne was one of few who would leave him some food in a tiny bowl. Sometimes she left a little cream or a small piece of salmon. She liked to see him bathe in the sunlight and turn over on his back to expose his belly. But today, a heavy gray sky and a few drips of quickening rain told of the coming storm. Adrianne opened the glass door to let the cat in.

"No need for you to get all wet," she whispered.

The cat meowed gratefully and slipped through the door, purred lightly, and rubbed against Adrianne's shin. She bent down to scratch him behind the ears.

.

.

.

```
>> reset /s envir.dat
>>
>>
```

The rain fell heavier, harder. The sky turned static gray. The cat backed away toward the stone wall. So did Adrianne. The falling water appeared like sheets of perfect white. Pellets of hail ting-ting-tinged against the windowpanes. Adrianne looked at the cat. The cat looked at her. If they could speak, they would both say, "What in the world is going on out there?"

Adrianne had not seen the weather reports today. She sensed it would rain, but not like this. The wind whipped violently. The scene outside the window was like a whirring blender. Trees, leaves, hail, water, dirt flew past. Then, as quickly as it had all begun, it ended. The trees in the courtyard were bent and broken. The plants lay on the ground.

Silence returned to the hall. It was interrupted by a ringing phone. Mother answered. Adrianne could hear her gravelly voice echo as if she gargled with sand every morning. Her words were muffled. Then she gasped.

Bad omens were everywhere.

Tornados had descended onto the city. Two funnels touched down near the water on the west side, mangling trees, throwing rocks, leaving destruction along their intoxicated paths. The Sisters tending the fire failed to keep the flame alive, and the mayor had been called in to relight it. The Sisters who had allowed the flame to go out were arrested.

Eight Sisters flanked the path to the entryway. Two were Sisters who were more than friends. One was the-girl-with-the-curly-red-hair-that-was-slowly-turning-auburn. One was Stephanie the brave. One was Helen. One was the-girl-with-the-gray-eyes-who-didn't-speak-too-much. One was the Mother. The last was Adrianne. A vigil in white flowing gowns. The drizzle steadily soaked through their clothing, the rain commingling with the water already on their faces.

No one spoke. Adrianne couldn't swallow as the van pulled up onto the wet cobblestone driveway. Helen and Adrianne's clasped hands hidden behind their robes. The sound of the side door sliding open felt like a knife piercing her chest. The four climbed out in handcuffs, wearing only white slips, exposing all their shame, shivering. There was only one other thing a Sister could do that was worse than this.

One of the four was Kimberly. Adrianne considered Kim a friend. They were not close, but still… Adrianne liked her. If only for a moment, their gazes met. Almost imperceptibly, Adrianne lifted her chin so that watching eyes wouldn't notice. Kim nodded in return. They were led inside and taken to one of the sublevels below to await judgment.

"What do you suppose they are going to do to them?" Helen whispered in a shaking voice once they reached their rooms upstairs.

"I don't know," Adrianne said.

"I read that they used to kill the girls who let the fire go out," Stephanie said.

"They won't," said the-girl-who-didn't-talk-too-much. "They can't… Can they?"

"That was a long time ago, Steph," Adrianne said.

"It's still possible," Stephanie said. "In wartime, people take the fire very seriously."

"The storm was bad. It could have happened to any one of us," Helen said.

The simple truth was finally stated. There was a freedom to the life they led. They could go shopping at the best stores, eat at the finest restaurants, go into the most elegant establishments in town—all without charge. But it was an illusion. They belonged to the state, and their lives were subject to the whims of chance. A freak storm had occurred. The eternal flame had gone out. Some-one had to pay. Someone had to be sacrificed.

It was the middle of the night when the Sisters were finally ushered down the stairs, past the levels where their guards lived, to a floor that Adrianne had only heard about and had never actu-ally seen. It was a humid, shadowy room lit with only candles. The Sisters formed a semicircle around four posts set in the middle of the floor. The wood looked new, as if cut recently.

Adrianne did her best not to seem scared. She had to show that she agreed with the punishment or risk sharing in it herself. In her mind she was flying up the stairs, out the door, and into the woods above. She was running and running and running so fast no one could catch her. She was the wind. She could take flight.

The four were unceremoniously dragged into the room. Thomas was one of the guards who dragged them to the posts. He looked up at Adrianne with fear in his eyes, even as he pulled at the struggling women. The guards tied them to the posts. The sounds of their whimpering tore at Adrian's insides. *I'll fly away, O Lord. I'll fly away...*

"*These* did the most heinous thing any of us could do," Mother said, letting her voice bounce off the high ceilings. "They let the light go out."

One of the girls shouted, "It was raining so hard!"

Another, "We tried everything we could...."

Another, "Please..."

Mother ignored their screams and said, "What is our duty? What is our most sacred duty?"

The Sisters spoke in unison, an automatic response like a trained muscle instilled in their minds from childhood, "To keep the flame alight."

"Cover their mouths," Mother said.

"No, please, don't—" one of them shouted, but no one would help. Everyone knew it. Even she knew it.

The guards did as they were told. This only made the four shout more, even as their mouths were gagged.

One great morning when the world is over, I'll fly away... away, away, so far away I'd fly, and no one would ever catch me.

"We have been too lax here of late," Mother said. "Perhaps the changes in our dress and the other new freedoms have led us to forget who and what we are. This is a time of war, Ladies. Our people look to us to be a shining example of our country's courage. We must never fail to keep the flame. It is our only purpose."

The air was charged with static that pricked the skin. Adrianne had no idea what was going to happen next. Each guard, including Thomas, stooped into the corner to pick up something. They reentered the circle and stood about six feet away from the posts. Adrianne squinted her eyes tight, trying to make out the objects in their hands. They were whips. The whites of Kim's eyes showed as a guard ripped off her slip, then that of the girl next to her, then the next, and the next.

Mother began to sing—*My country, 'tis of thee...*

The rest of the Order joined in, singing lightly in shaking soprano—*Sweet land of Liberty...*

The first lash sent red rippling. The splatter of it stained white robes. A scream, even through the cloth tied around their mouths, pierced the ears and filled the room. Mother sang louder to cover the echo—*Of thee I sing...*

The second lash—*Land where my fathers died*

The third—the fourth—*Land of the Romans' pride*

Lash after lash after lash after lash—*From every mountainside Let freedom ring...*

"So, are they dead?"

"No," Adrianne said. "But I'm sure they wish they were."

Antoine ran his fingers through her dreads and kissed her exposed shoulder. Then he pulled up the blanket to warm her.

"I didn't think they did things like that anymore."

"They do. I saw it with my own eyes."

"I'm sorry you had to go through that."

"It wasn't me that went through it."

The silence the Sisters lived in was now filled with a sense of terror. Their steps were more careful. Their gowns more starched and sparkling white. Mistakes were hidden more quickly. And the fire blazed hotter and brighter. To escape watchful eyes, Adrianne had used every trick of evasion to get to the room where Antoine was waiting—their special place of hiding—their place of love—that felt more and more like a tomb. She folded into his arms, feeling safe for only brief moments. Then the fear would filter through again and cover all they had in a thick black cloud.

"I leave tomorrow. We're being shipped out."

Adrianne rolled over to face away from him.

"I'll be back as soon as I can," he said.

"I know."

"Maybe it's better if I'm away."

"How do you mean?"

"It will be safer for you. Less chances to take for a while."

Adrianne didn't know what to say to that. It had been on her mind. Thoughts of him being so far away, of him running from bullets, or being blown up in his vehicle swarmed in her mind. She hugged herself tighter.

"You're being awfully quiet about this," he said.

"What do you want me to say?"

"What are you thinking?"

"I'm thinking about the fire going out," she lied. "They say that it is a bad omen for the war."

"Adrianne, do you honestly think that what you do in that park makes a hell of a difference when I'm out there getting shot at?"

"No.... Maybe.... I don't know...." she said.

"The war is already going badly. It might even—" He stopped mid-sentence and nuzzled her hair.

"It might even what?"

"It might even reach our shores someday."

Adrianne thought about this for a moment, then dismissed the idea. Antoine could be so melodramatic sometimes. She turned over and faced him.

"I wish you would get away from that crazy cult you're in," he said.

"Antoine, I wish you would stop saying that. You know that it's impossible. And breaking my vows would be wrong."

"Then what is *this*? Isn't this breaking your vows?"

She swallowed, "I suppose, but this is different."

"How is this different?"

"It just is...." she said. "Besides, it's not so easy to leave. You know that. There is nowhere to go."

"Maybe we could smuggle you up north. Maybe we could go together."

Silence.

"Adrianne, one day you're going to have to admit to yourself that this is not who you are. This is not what you want to be."

"Don't tell me what I want," Adrianne said and got out of bed. She searched for her clothes that lay on the floor. Antoine put his hand on her bare back and gently brought her into his arms again, then under the sheets. He kissed her tenderly on the shoulder and said, "I'm sorry. We don't have to talk about it anymore." He turned her over on her back. He kissed her again on the forehead, then the cheek, then the neck. He firmly put her leg to one side. She didn't resist. He entered her and she felt the fullness of him. The weight of him. The slip of him. The pull. The thrust. The ache. The smell. The moan. He was hers, she was his. They were one.

Adrianne walked out to the harbor. In the distance, the crescent moon sprinkled light on the water. A dot of green flickered in the night sky. The tide had gone out, leaving mud below the dock. A slight breeze moved the fishy sweet air. Surrounded by shades and the irregular shapes of boxes and abandoned storage equipment, Adrianne felt a chill, then covered herself. Antoine had left a half an hour ago. Now it was her turn. Thomas would make sure she got home.

"Thom," she called. No answer.

"Thom?" she repeated. Still, no answer.

Adrianne stepped over the broken boards.

"Thom?" she whispered.

"Hey," someone said, "you're out pretty late."

Adrianne couldn't see the source of the disembodied male voice. It came from behind a stack of old crates. She decided not to answer, only to move faster.

"Where ya going, sista? Somewhere you need to be?"

The voice was right behind her. She could feel its male bulk following her. She was easy prey. Exposed. Helpless. Before her moved the shadows of several men.

"Run, Adrianne!" Thomas called. His voice was cut off by the sound of meat being pounded, then a loud bang. Adrianne scrambled frantically. Her robes twisted about her legs, almost making her trip. She held up her dress so she could run faster. She looked around, went to the edge of the pier, and jumped. She fell wrong on her foot, onto wet soil. Above her, running feet scuffled on the wooden planks. Her ankle hurt like hell, but she had to keep moving. She was surrounded by reeds and slimy, smelly, nasty things. She had no time to think or feel or be scared. She moved silently among the leaves. Flashlights peered down from the dock to find her.

Her white robe was sullied with mud and muck as she went deeper and deeper into the reeds. Someone jumped down from the pier, then someone else. She kept moving. Then a flashlight found her. The men grabbed her. She fought like a cat. A wet cloth with a sweet chemical smell covered her mouth. And all went dark.

Adrianne woke to light and colors with unfocused edges. She blinked several times and still she could not see clearly. She had a terrible headache, one that she felt in her ears and on the bridge of her nose. The fuzziness focused. Twelve Sisters were in the room. A vigil in white flowing gowns. Four were the Sisters who were best friends. Two were Sisters who were more than that. One was the-girl-with-the-curly-red-hair-that-was-slowly-turning-auburn. One was Stephanie the brave. One was Helen. One was the-girl-with-the-gray-eyes-who-didn't-speak-too-much. One was the Mother. The last was Adrianne. Ten Sisters held each other. Helen stood alone with skin as pale as her white robe.

"Of all the girls I never thought it would be you."

"Mother?" Adrianne said.

Mother slapped her hard across the face.

"Don't call me that, you little whore." Adrianne tried to move her hands. They were tied together.

"The little brown girl with the big brown eyes. So innocent. So pure. You were actually one of my favorites."

Helen whimpered, water flowing down her face.

"I remember when your mother brought you here. We normally wouldn't take a girl like you. We only take girls from the best families to serve with us. But she'd been beaten by a man, and I felt sorry for her. She said you were good. So I made an exception. Now look at you.... Nothing to say?"

Adrianne swallowed.

"Lower her."

Adrianne felt the floor beneath her going down.

"What's happening?"

"Don't you know what we do to little girls who can't keep their legs closed?"

The chair Adrianne was tied to rocked a little as she shook it with all her might. It remained firmly secured on the plank as she was lowered into the open grave. She went down and down and down until the ground came up to her waist, then her bust.

"And don't worry about your boyfriend. Antoine is dead. We threw his body into the river last night."

"No..." she whispered. The air escaped her lungs. "No..."

The smell of the moist, cool earth surrounded her. In those last few moments when she could still see her Sisters and the Mother, her urge to scream faded. Antoine was dead, and so to die was of little consequence. And a few things that had been a mystery, now seemed so clear.

She said in a calm voice as a heavy slab of granite was slowly rolled overhead, "You are wrong to do this and one day you will know." The light slipped away from the edges of the slab as they were sealed by the mason workers. The scraping sounds of the cement being smoothed and finished echoed in the emptiness of her tomb.

There was very little air now. Adrianne swooned and woke moments later to the blackness. She thought then that it was best to go back to sleep. Maybe when she woke again, she would find herself in the arms of the one she loved.

6.

```
>>
>> suspend

** SYSTEM SUSPENDED **

>> run diagnostics
    .
    .
    .


*DIAGNOSTICS COMPLETE*

==> ERRORS FOUND: FRAGMENTATION @ SECTOR: 10110001

RUNNING REPAIRS
    .
    .
    .
```

"Adrianne...Adrianne...can you hear me?" The doctor waved his fingers before her eyes, then took some notes. "Reduce her dosage by 25 milligrams. Maybe tomorrow she'll be more responsive."

```
*ERRORS LOCALIZED*
    .
    .
    .
```

"Adrianne...Adrianne?" the doctor said.
She turned her eyes toward him.
"Blink if you understand me."
She blinked.
"Do you know where you are? Blink once for yes, twice for no."

She blinked twice.

"You're in a hospital. We are taking good care of you. Don't worry, just rest."

He tapped her on the arm and smiled grimly. She felt feverish inside her skull, as if she were smoldering behind her face. Heavy, drowsy. Her head turned, her consciousness followed moments later. Cool lids closed over hot eyes. Slowly she drifted back to sleep.

```
>>
>> system reset
.

.

.
```

"How are you doing today?"
"Better."
"Good, good."

```
.

.

.
```

It was a warm day, and the patients were allowed outside. They wore soft hospital gowns that were almost white, but upon closer inspection they were light blue. Some with stripes. Some with paisleys. Some with tiny wildflowers. The patients roamed this section of the grounds in sight of the staff. Some stood still with sun on their faces. Being locked up made the warmth of it feel like heaven. Trees surrounded the neatly kept lawn, and chairs painted a crisp white sat lonely among them. Adrianne found a plot of soft grass and sat down. Wet soaked through her gown to her butt. She didn't care. She liked the smell of the grass. Her mind drifted off to the place it had been going more and more lately. She was in her safe place.

Behind her loomed a large brick mansion with a large porch bordered by Corinthian columns. It was a home for those who couldn't cope on the outside.

"Adrianne, how are you feeling today?" a doctor asked.

"Fine," Adrianne said, not facing him.

"Adrianne, my name is Dr. Tomas. I have been assigned to your case."

The wind smelled good, sweet like newly fallen rain. She felt him sit down in the chair next to her and wondered what he looked like, though not enough to turn around and see for herself.

"Could you tell me why you did it?" He waited for an answer that did not come. "Adrianne, why did you try to kill yourself?"

"I didn't."

"Yes, you did."

"No, I didn't."

"If we are to make any progress, you will need to be honest—"

Adrianne heard his words and ignored their meaning. It was the way of things, she thought. People talk and talk and say silly things that don't mean anything.

"War is coming," she said.

"What?"

"War is coming."

She turned around and faced him for the first time. He was young. Too young to be a doctor, she thought. And on this side of handsome. She stood for a moment to gaze at the trees whose boughs swayed gently in the breeze. Something rustled in the wet leaves covering the ground—a small rabbit, sitting on its hindquarters, nibbling on a stalk of grass. As she watched, it hopped away, disappearing into a hole it had dug somewhere.

"A war is coming..."

In a comfortable living room–style lounge with a ping-pong table off to the side, a nice setting with heavy locks and bars on the windows and a basketball game on the television, a man with salt-and-pepper hair, who seemed as though he belonged at home playing with his grandchildren, sat in front of the set. People, young and old and of every shade and description, roamed around. Some looked visibly frightened, others looked tired. Adrianne sat by herself, staring into that far-off place in her mind again. She thought in numbers.

One zero one one zero zero zero one one zero one one zero zero zero one one zero one one zero zero zero one...

"There's some crazy ass motherfuckers up in *here*!" Hector laughed. He wore ill-fitting Daisy Dukes with thick unshaven legs and held a hairbrush.

"Hey, honey. What you doing?" He pointed to Adrianne with his brush, then smoothed it over his shoulder-length hair that was tousled even though he constantly brushed it.

...one zero one one zero zero zero one one zero one one zero zero zero one one zero one one zero zero zero one...

"Okay, honey. Whatever. Stare into space for all I care." Hector waved his brush in Adrianne's face, then sat down. "Shove over a bit, sweetie, so I can sit, gee." Adrianne moved.

...one zero zero zero one one zero one one zero zero zero one one zero one one zero zero zero one...

"You're new. What you in here for?" Hector asked. "No, wait, let me guess...schizo, right? Or, bipolar with complications." Hector laughed. "Lawd, those damn complications will get you every time!" He brushed his hair. "Me? Well, honey, I'm not here for the reason you think. Yes, I *am* a transsexual, thank you. Not a transvestite. That's a whole nother thing. I don't mess around in women's clothes 'cus I like it. I *am* an actual woman. God just gave me a little something extra at birth, which ain't none of your damn business. But they think I need to get my head straight, s'cuse the pun. It was all that crying I did after my momma passed. They say that I can't take care of myself."

...zero one one zero one one zero zero zero one one zero one one zero zero zero one one zero one one zero...

"But I know better, though." Hector stopped brushing his hair. "Right, Little Stevie?"

"Yes, right. You're right. You're always right," Little Stevie said as he sat in front of the television.

"I mean, crying after your momma dies is normal, isn't it? It's as normal as 1-2-3. You're supposed to cry when you lose somebody special, right? Well, these suckers think it was a sign that something was wrong. So what, I cried for a few months? Ain't nothing wrong with me, honey. I know who I am. I was just born into the wrong body, that's all. And my momma was the only one that understood. The only one that mattered..." Hector went back to brushing his hair. "Right, Little Stevie?"

"Yes, right. You're right. You're always right," Little Stevie said.

...one one zero zero zero one one zero one one zero zero zero one one zero one one zero zero zero one...

"Now they got me on these happy pills." Hector did a wiggle dance with his butt on the couch next to Adrianne. "Woo! Love them happy pills."

"War is coming."

"What you say, honey?"

"War is coming."

"War is coming? As far as I can see, war is already *here!*" Hector blurted with a fake laugh. "Right, Little Stevie?"

"Yes, right. You're right. You're always right," Little Stevie said.

"Oh, yes, you gotta fight through this life, girl. Every day, every day. Every-single-day is a battle, chile."

...one zero one one zero zero zero one one zero one one zero zero zero one ...

"You know what? I like you. You wanna be my friend, honey?" Hector said, gently poking Adrianne with his hairbrush.

"You're already my friend, Helen."

...one zero one one zero zero zero one one zero one one zero zero zero one...

"What did you just say?" Hector poked her some more with his brush. "What did you just call me?" Hector bopped her hard with the brush.

Adrianne focused for the first time in days. "Helen, you didn't have to hit me. I said that I was your friend."

Hector stood up. "God, how you know my name? Only my momma knows my name! And she's dead. Dead, dead, dead. Chile, how you know my name?"

The orderlies came over. They were bulky men who grabbed Hector by both arms.

"Come on, Hector. Leave her alone."

"No, but she knows my name."

"We know your name, too, Hector. It's time for your pill."

"No," he said. "How you know my name, honey? You know my name," Hector said as he was taken away. "But she knows my name. Honey, how you know my name?"

...zero one one zero one one zero zero zero one one zero one one zero zero zero one one zero one one zero...

```
>>
>>
>> opendialog SECTOR: 10110001

: How are you doing?
```
  "What?"
```
: I said, how are you doing?
```
  "You tell me."
```
: You seem troubled.
```
  "I'm not troubled. Just tired."
```
: Get some rest. It will be better soon.
```
  "Who the hell are you anyway? And how are you in my head?"
```
: end;
>>
>> continue

BRIDGE PROCESS: CONTINUED
```
   .
   .

   .

"How are you doing?"

"Why do you keep asking me that? You are always in my head."

Dr. Tomas took down some notes on his clipboard.

"We want to try something with you that we think might help."

"Are you asking me for permission or telling me what you are going to do?"

He took down some notes.

"You seem more aware today. That's good."

Adrianne scanned the office. Pictures of the doctor's children and of his new bride on their wedding day sat on his desk. A framed painting on the wall overshadowed the room. It was of a man sailing a boat along a river and an elk staring up from the bushes to the side.

"I know that man."

"What man?"

"The man in the painting. Someone should tell him he's in trouble on that water."

The doctor took down some more notes.

"Adrianne, why don't we try to talk some more about why you are here?"

She focused more on the painting, following the flow of the acrylic waters that sparkled with dots of white from the yellow-orange sun and the curious elk in the bushes who seemed to blink.

"Well?"

"Well, what?"

"Do you want to talk about it?"

"There's nothing to say."

"You tried to hurt yourself."

"That's not how I remember it."

"How do you remember it then?"

Adrianne stared past the doctor and studied the two big filing cabinets that stood guard by the door, holding the secrets of many deranged minds. Adrianne wondered if the stories they held were real or as imagined as everything else around her.

"Adrianne, how do you remember it?"

Adrianne looked Dr. Tomas in the eyes. "I don't remember it," she lied, "but I know that I didn't hurt myself."

The doctor wrote something down on his clipboard.

"You said before that 'War is coming.' What did you mean by that?"

"Just what I said."

"What war do you mean?"

Silence.

Dr. Tomas looked off into space for a minute, considering.

"Tell me about Antoine."

A twinge of pain. A raised eyebrow.

"What do you want to know?"

"You seemed to have cared for him quite a bit."

Silence.

"His death must have been a very painful experience for you."

Again silence.

"Tell me about him. What was he like?"

...zero one one zero one one zero zero zero one one zero one one zero zero zero one one zero one one zero...

"Adrianne?" The doctor wrote something down.

"Adrianne, there is a new medication that I would like to give to you. I think it may help you moderate your moods."

Adrianne concentrated on the light streaming through the barred window that sent shadows to the walls in shapes of grids and lines. The color of the curtains was a shade of cream fit for pouring into coffee. The smell of artificial lemon and pine furniture wax permeated the air and made her feel woozy.

"Thomas, I know you're only trying to help. Do what you think is best."

```
** BREAK **
>>
>>
>> createdoc defrag.fi

# defrag.fi -- defragments a life span
# by compressing it segment by segment

init  time, place;
init  life_span;
init  segment = _get(param[0]);

life_span = getLifespan (segment);
place = getLocation (life_span);

print "** Defragging..." ;

while (life_span)
{
    if ( fragmented (life_span)) then
    {
        time = getTimeLine (life_span);
        life_span = _compress (time, place);
```

```
        life_span = getNextLifespan (life_
        span);
    }
    else break;
}
return print "**Lifespan Defragmentation Complete";
.eof

>>
>>
>> execute defrag 177

** Defragging...
```

Adrian sat in the back of the room, eyes wide open in the dark. Dr. Tomas looked in on him through a slit in the door. They stared each other down. Predator to prey.

"How are you doing today?"

In a low whisper Adrian answered, "Why don't you come in here and find out?"

A cold chill.

"Would you like me to come inside?"

"Yes," Adrian said calmly, "that way I can pluck your eyes out of their sockets, doctor."

Dr. Tomas closed the slit on the door and turned to the orderly. "Increase his medication."

```
>>
>> process -b
        [1]    01110001       04:31:02
        [2]    10101100       10:52:49
        [3]    10110001       00:00:00
        [4]    10101011       53:45:13
        [5]    10010101       34:38:24
    .

    .
>> kill [3]
>> kill [3]
>> kill [3]
>>
>>
```

"Adrian, this is Dr. Tomas. Can you hear me?"

A snarl vibrated from behind the locked door. Adrian sounded like a large cat with teeth made for rending flesh. He hissed, then went quiet like a menacing dark spirit in the back of the cell.

"How long has he been like this?"

"All night."

A growl, low and intense.

"This is not working." He wrote out a new script. "Stop the medication and give him this."

```
>> kill -1 [3]

*PROCESS 10110001 TERMINATED*
>> clear
 .

 .

 .

**Lifespan Defragmentation Complete

>>
>> restart process 10110001

*PROCESS 10110001 RESTARTED*

>>
 .

 .

 .
```

7.

Antoine walked across the wet cobblestone driveway toward the modern wing of the hospital. He wore a military-issue jacket and heavy boots, fresh home from his stint overseas. The sky was clear and moist after a mid-morning shower. He pulled up his collar and ducked his head. As he approached the hospital, he faced his reflection in the glass doors and saw what others saw. He was very good-looking, a condition of birth. It hadn't made the struggles of his recent years any easier, his pain any less, or his burdens any lighter.

A flutter flutter of wings in the trees made him look up. The birds that had gathered in the branches were rustling the leaves. A sudden gust of wind forced them to take flight, filling the blue sky with a parade of flapping black sideways parentheses. In the distance, he saw the spires of the city and above them, a mist falling down. From where he stood, the sky directly overhead hung a calm and beautiful blue.

Antoine passed through the first set of glass doors into the vestibule and glanced in disgust at the names of the wealthy donors on the plaque on the wall. He snorted and moved through the inner set of doors and into the lobby. Brown plaid cushions on faux wooden chairs and a coffee table with scattered magazines furnished the room. Reprints of museum watercolors adorned the walls. Antoine approached the desk. The young woman sitting there barely acknowledged him, until the beauty of the clean-shaven statuesque man registered. Then a huge taunting smile appeared on her face. He had her full attention.

"May I help you?" she said.

"I'm looking for my brother. I was told that he was taken here."

"Okay," she said. "May I have his name?" She turned to her terminal while somehow still keeping her gaze on Antoine.

"His name is Adrian—"

The phone interrupted them. Then another call a second later. Then more calls. The receptionist put up a finger as she tried to answer them all, placing most on hold. Antoine struggled to remain calm. He knew why the calls were coming in. Anyone who had looked outside knew. But evidently those in their cozy little jobs in their cozy little offices remained oblivious to what had just happened only a few miles away. His heart thumped hard, and he could feel the blood reaching toward his face. He paced the floor, waiting for the receptionist to get off the phone. This was a waste of time, he thought. A rumbling like thunder rolled outside. The floor shook. Antoine grabbed hold of the receptionist's desk to catch his balance.

Antoine's patience had evaporated. He marched to the locked double doors marked "Staff Only" and slipped through when they opened to let a nurse out.

Doors and doors and more doors lined the corridors. He heard the receptionist call from behind, "Sir! Sir! You can't go back there!" Antoine ignored her as well as the heads poking out of the offices that watched him pass. His only concern was Adrian. Had he known that while he was away this would happen—that his little brother would be taken to a place like this—maybe he wouldn't have gone. Maybe.

He walked faster as the quickened clicks of heels on the linoleum tile trailed behind him.

"Sir! Sir! You can't be back here!"

He pushed open a door. Behind it was a group of patients gathered in a circle of chairs. They calmly looked up, unperturbed by his presence, only curious. Life had worn them down—the sudden appearance of Antoine was of little concern.

"Sir! Sir!" he heard from behind.

He continued walking.

"Adrian!" he called. "It's Antoine! Where are you?"

He looked through another door. When he turned he found that he was surrounded by orderlies and security.

"Sir, you can't be back here," the receptionist said as she reached out to touch Antoine's arm. She pulled back in the last moment, her eyes wide with fear.

"I wanna see my brother."

"Come this way and we will try and help you," a man said and waved him towards the lobby.

Antoine looked around him. The men were big. But Antoine was bigger and meaner and more desperate. Each breath was hard and paced. There were two ways to get out of this. He could return to the reception area or he could punch his way through. He curled his fingers into a fist hidden beneath his jacket sleeve. Then the building started to shake again and the ground trembled violently. Everyone in the hall moved to brace themselves. A snaking crack snapped open on the wall near the ceiling, sprinkling dust onto the heads of those nearby. The lights went out, then came back on a moment later.

It was happening. It was coming.

"What was that?" the receptionist said, her voice an octave higher.

"While you're figuring that out, I'm getting my brother."

"Wait—"

Antoine pushed past the dazed staff and ran.

His calls were swallowed by the calls of others. Doctors and nurses, janitors and staff panicked as the ground continued to vibrate. They screamed out to each other, confused and scared. Patients entered the hallway only to be ushered back into their rooms.

The ground continued to move. As Antoine rushed about, the voices of the orderlies and receptionist echoed far behind him. The lights flickered off, and there was a heartbeat spent in pitch black, stillness. Dim emergency lights flooded the halls with an orange glow, and the bedlam resumed.

"Adrian!" Antoine called. "Adrian!"

He peered into a room to find a group of patients with terrified expressions stirring nervously as a lone staff person attempted to calm them. Antoine returned to the hall and grabbed by the arm someone who was running.

"I'm looking for a man."

"Aren't we all." Hector shook off his grip. "Now get off!" Hector turned back into his room and tried to close the door. Antoine grabbed at his arm again.

"I'm looking for Adrian"

"Adrian?" Hector looked strangely at him through the crack of the door. "What you want him for?"

"He's my brother and I'm getting him outta here."

Hector said, "Well, you can't be his brother. His brother's dead."

"Who told you that?"

"Shh! Keep your voice down." Hector pulled him inside the room just in time to hide from the approaching security guard.

"Who told you that?" Antoine repeated in a quieter voice.

"Adrian did."

"*Where* is he?!" Antoine grabbed Hector's arms.

"Ow! Honey, that hurts!"

"It'll hurt even more if you don't tell me where my brother is."

"How do I know you're really his brother?"

"I don't have time to fuck around!"

"Do I look like I'm fuckin' around to you?" Hector said, shaking himself loose. "It don't take no genius to see something bad is going down. Now prove to me you're his brother."

Antoine thought for a minute then said, "He has a mark on his forehead from when he was in an accident with some scaffolding."

Hector pursed his lips. "Anyone who's seen him can say that."

"He likes owls," Antoine said exasperated. "Come on, Nut!" Antoine shoved Hector.

"Alright, alright, I can show you!" Hector said. "But you gotta promise that when you're leaving you take me, too."

Antoine took a moment to consider the vision of Hector in his tight blue jeans, lady's slippers, long hair, and moustache. He decided that he'd let him show him where Adrian was, then dump him afterwards.

"Fine. Whatever, Nut. Show me."

Hector smiled and disappeared into his closet for a moment and returned with a small purse.

"Come on, honey. Time's a wastin'. And my name is Hector, not Nut."

Hector stuck his head out the door and looked both ways, then waved for Antoine to follow. Alarms were honking, and an automated voice blared instructions to remain calm. They slipped along the halls together, unnoticed by the rushing staff who had their hands full dealing with running patients. Antoine followed Hector to a locked door. Hector took a card out of his purse and swiped it through the security lock.

"I stole this from an orderly weeks ago. He never missed it. He so stupid."

The door opened to a stairwell that led downstairs. The noise from the hall cut off when the door behind them slammed shut. The faded red glow of the exit sign provided a little light. Antoine followed Hector down the stairs to the lower level, into a maze of dark corridors that smelled of floor cleaner, a sickly sweet scent of pine and ammonia.

"Over here," Hector said.

Antoine hesitated, doubling his fists. It occurred to him that it might be dangerous to follow a mental patient into the dark when he had no idea where he was going. Then Hector stopped at a door and gently knocked.

"Adrian, it's me."

Hector pulled something else out of his purse and began working at the knob. "Give me a minute," he said. It was silent enough for Antoine to hear the metal gears of the lock move, then snap into place.

"There," Hector said and pushed the door slowly open. If it was dim in the hallway, it was like a void in that room. Hector went inside without hesitation. Antoine remained by the door and slowly opened it more until he could see what was inside. Squinting, he could just make out something lying in the corner. Hector was sitting next to it.

"Oh, Papi, what they do to you this time?" Hector said.

Antoine felt a pull. He didn't want to believe it. He wanted this Hector guy to be a mental case that he could smack in the next two seconds. Antoine went inside and moved closer, then bent down. In the blackness he could barely make out the bearded man, lying semi-comatose, as Hector wiped drool from his mouth.

"I've been coming down here whenever I can to visit. Let him know that he wasn't alone. The stuff they do to him here…"

Hector pointed to his temple. "You're lucky if there's anyone left upstairs."

Antoine felt a flush of gratitude. Hector had done what he himself should have done—taken care of his brother.

Antoine touched Adrian's face and felt his coarse facial hair on his fingertips and the drool flowing from the corner of his mouth. *Dear God, what have they been doing to you?*

"Helen," Adrian whispered.

"Yeah, honey, it's me," Hector said. "This guy here says he's your brother."

"Antoine..."

"Yeah, it's me, bro," Antoine said and pulled Adrian into his arms. "I didn't know they put you in a place like this. I would've never have let them do this to you. Damn, Adrian, I'm sorry. I'm so so sorry...." He buried his face between Adrian's neck and shoulder.

"This is beautiful and all, but don't we gotta leave?" Hector said.

"Yeah," Antoine said as he wiped his brother's cheek with his thumb. He lifted him up and placed Adrian's arm around his shoulder. Hector took Adrian's other arm around his shoulder, and together they all stumbled out the door.

"What's happening?" Adrian asked.

"I'm takin' you away from here," Antoine said.

They groped their way back down the empty hall. Muffled shouts and screams and the vibrations of the earth could be heard in the cinderblock hallway. They struggled up the stairwell with Adrian's dead weight. His head bobbed back and forth. Antoine leaned against the doorframe with his brother in his arms and waited as Hector opened the door into a hallway chaotic with blaring horns and staffers ushering patients into rooms. The three were able to slip through it all, heading toward the glowing red exit sign that led to the lobby.

"Hey, you can't go out there!"

They didn't stop or turn around. They walked faster. The security guard slapped Antoine on the shoulder and pulled him around. Antoine shoved Adrian into Hector's arms and punched the guard square in the face. The blare of horns, the murmur of confused voices, the scrambling of feet hid the sound of the smack. Blood squirted from the guard's nose as he doubled over, then fell to his knees.

"Come on!" Antoine shouted to Hector and grabbed Adrian's arm again. Hector moved quickly to keep up. An acrid smell of ash and smoke, of burning fuel or melting metal, had seeped into the lobby. The receptionist stood by her desk with her hand covering her mouth and nose. The ground still moved beneath their feet, but it now felt more like the vibrations from a large passing truck than an earthquake.

"Cover your face," Antoine said as he pulled his shirt over his mouth and nose. He stopped to wrap his scarf around Adrian's head, leaving only his eyes exposed.

"Maybe we shouldn't go out there," Hector said.

"We need to get out of here," Antoine said. He opened the door. The sky above them remained a quiet clear blue.

"What's that smell?"

Antoine didn't answer. Adrian mumbled something incoherent as they hurried through a swirling mist that gathered around their feet that turned and moved almost as if it were alive. They ran to Antoine's truck parked on the other side of the street. A miasma rose in the distance and the smell was danker. Antoine opened the passenger side door and together he and Hector put Adrian into the back seat. Antoine took a moment to examine Hector. He was about to shove this weird guy to the ground, but then he remembered the loving way Hector had touched his brother in that dark room. Antoine moved to let Hector climb into the passenger seat while he went to the driver's side.

"Where we goin'?" Hector asked once they were on their way.

"Somewhere that's not here."

Ahead of them, a dense cloud was rising. Antoine depended on his memory of the road to drive. Hector mumbled to himself. Every so often Antoine heard him utter words that sounded like "Heh-zeuz," "Chris-toh," and "De-ohs."

"Helen?" Adrian said in a dreamy voice from the back seat.

"Yes, Papi," Hector called back.

"I dreamt I saw my brother again."

"Go back to sleep, okay, honey."

"You'll be here when I wake up?"

"Don't worry, Helen's here, Papi. We be alright," Hector calmly said as he crossed himself.

The sky was streaked with pink as the orange sun dipped into the breast of the earth. A green speck shimmered near the horizon. As they drove they saw more and more cars speeding past them, all going in the other direction. The cloud. The mist. The nothing was spreading. It ate everything it encountered. And yet they were driving right into it.

"Shouldn't we be going the other way?" Hector begged.

"No, it's safer to go into the center."

"Wha, you crazy?"

"Don't distract me right now," Antoine said through gritted teeth. It had been a long day, and there was no end in sight. Adrian was all that mattered, and he was lying in the back seat. Antoine had to take him someplace safe. He wasn't quite sure where that place was.

Antoine pulled over into the breakdown lane and parked. He covered his face with his shirt again and got out of the truck. He stood outside the driver's side door, staring beyond the sparse trees along the highway, into a clear view of a skyline of tall skyscrapers. The squawks of birds echoed overhead as they flew to escape to places unknown. Antoine slammed the truck door shut and went into the trees to relieve himself. Mist descended into the foliage around him. He felt as if he had entered a dream world. He finished and zipped his pants. Antoine turned around to see an elk among the trees. They stared at each other for a long moment, then the elk wandered into the mist and disappeared.

He returned to the truck and found Hector talking over the seat to a more awake Adrian.

"See, I told you he was here," Hector said.

"Antoine?" Adrian said. Then his eyes rolled back into his head, and he leaned sideways. Hector struggled to make sure he landed safely on the seat cushion.

"I don't think he's ready to see you yet," Hector said. "Where you been anyway? This poor kid thought you were dead."

"I nearly was—"

Out of the blue, blue sky a ship flew. It was too fast to be a plane. Then there were more of them. They raced as though piloted by madmen. Their exhaust lines streaked the air in their wake like sheet music. Silver and shiny and soundless, the ships soared directly into the city and slammed into the two highest buildings. Orange plumes mixed with black smoke blossoming into the air.

```
*DELETING FILES*

deleting: /system/kernel/ui/ras/environment/...
deleting: /system/kernel/ui/ras/environment/.../
staging/...
deleting: /system/kernel/ui/ras/environment/.../.../
ui/...
deleting: /system/kernel/ui/ras/environment/.../
view/...
deleting: /system/kernel/ui/ras/environment/.../
view/ui/...
** BREAK **
** BREAK **

>> abort

*ABORT IGNORED*

deleting: /system/kernel/ui/ras/environment/...
deleting: /system/kernel/network/ras/env/.../
staging/...
deleting: /system/kernel/network/ras/env/.../
staging/ui/...
deleting: /system/kernel/network/ras/env/.../view/...
deleting: /system/kernel/network/ras/env/.../view/
ui/...
deleting: /system/kernel/network/ras/env/.../.../...
  .
  .
  .
```

"Day-um!" Hector yelled with a shaking pointer finger.

The tallest buildings collapsed, falling down like playing cards. The whole skyline seemed to disappear as smoke billowed upwards, the city dissolving into a sea of dust.

"What is going on?!" Hector cried.

Antoine said, "It's the war come home."

He had seen it when he was over there. They were spreading the dust before they slammed into the buildings. And the dust would change things. It would change people. It would spread outwards to cover everything with its nothingness. He'd be damned if he'd let that happen to his brother. Antoine got back into the truck and started the engine.

"Where we going?"

"To the city."

"Nah uh! Oh no, honey! Not me!"

Hector was reaching to open his door when Antoine grabbed his hand. He was gentle but his eyes were intense.

"We can stay in the truck until some of the smoke clears, but then we have to go into the city. They'll be building a safe place there. They've been doing the same thing in all the major cities overseas. Trust me, I know. We'll be safer in the city."

Hector looked around at the nothingness outside and then at Adrian sleeping in the back seat. He swallowed hard, then nodded.

8.

A city can be silent only when something is not right. The wrongness of the world seeped into the truck along with the bad smell. They had spent three days sleeping on the road, and now they were going into the center of the metropolis. Smoke hovered over the water, making the city appear as though it floated on a cloud. Its crumbling buildings jutted into the air like broken teeth. The lights that once glittered in the night were gone, making the skyline seem draped in shadow.

They crossed over the gothic bridge that rose high above the river. Its cables strained under the weight of all the cars, trucks, and people on it. They drove slowly past those who walked with their faces covered with makeshift masks of ripped clothes or handkerchiefs or bandanas, a parade of the confused covered in dust and the debris of fallen buildings. These were the survivors trying to get home, if home was still there. There was nothing anyone could do. Night was coming, and soon it would be hard to see. God help them if it started to rain.

Before Antoine, Adrian, and Hector was a city in chaos. Buildings were missing and so were people. An eerie scene lay before them of emptiness where things used to be and quiet where the noise of a million voices once filled the air. Adrian was jostled and felt every bump and curve of the road they traveled. He lifted his head, feeling its enormous weight, and it throbbed in time with his pulse. In front of him, he could see that Antoine's shoulders were tense. His fingers gripped the steering wheel as if he could pull it out of its base. Adrian had for so long believed his brother dead that seeing him again was like a wild unbelievable dream. The presence of the beautiful boy who swooped down as if on eagle's wings to pluck him out of the depths filled him with a simultaneous sense of joy and foreboding. He had so many things he wanted to say to his brother. So many words that had formed in his mind. But he held back from speaking.

"I'm hungry," Hector said.

"Yeah, me too," Antoine said and pulled the truck over in front of a small supermarket. Its sign shined a hazy light through the settling dust. A gray shutter-gate was pulled down over the storefront's window, padlocks clamped on either side. Antoine went to the back of the truck and pulled out a crowbar. Hector watched him, shaking his head.

"Papi, I think your brother will make trouble for us."

Adrian sat up and watched as Antoine banged at the locks to the gate. He eventually broke them open and threw the gate up with a loud slam. When he returned to the truck he tossed the crowbar into the back.

"You know, you shouldn't break into other people's shit."

"There's no one here."

"That doesn't make it right."

"Whatever. I'm getting something to eat. Besides we shouldn't stay out here tonight. Help me get him inside."

Hector pursed his lips, but did what he was told and helped to lift the groggy Adrian out of the truck and into the market.

In the corner between the baby things and the feminine hygiene products, where it smelled of oversweet powder and deodorant, they set Adrian down. Hector made a bed out of packages of diapers and watched Adrian curl up in them. He was caressing Adrian's sleeping head when the lights turned on.

"I found the power switches," Antoine shouted from behind a wall.

The store had not been abandoned long. The milk was still cold, and there were plenty of canned goods, packages of dried snacks, and preserved foods in salt and bottles of brine. The refrigerators and their compressors huffed and puffed like overweight children. It felt wrong to just take things off the shelves and open them, but that's what Hector did. A package of peanuts, a bag of chips, a can of soda—then he changed his mind and went for a carton of chocolate milk. Antoine roamed the aisles taking food from the shelves, crinkling bags open and munching as he went. The cocking of a gun caught everyone's attention.

"What are you doing in my store?" a voice said.

Frozen. Speechless. Guilty.

Appearing from a doorway was a man shakily holding a big black gun. He was small and middle-aged and skinny. Dangling at the side of his neck was a dust mask. His hand might have been nervous, but his face was firm.

"This is my store."

"We didn't know," Hector said with a half-eaten bag of peanuts in his hand.

"You knew it was *somebody's* store."

"Everyone's gone," Antoine said. "We didn't think anyone was here."

"This is my store. I don't leave my own store," the man said.

"We didn't take much," Hector said. "We can leave."

The store owner wore an expression that was a mixture of skepticism and relief.

"You're the Mr. Kim from the sign, right?" Antoine said.

"Yes, I'm Mr. Kim and this is *my* store. I build this store. I make my business. This is my home upstairs. No one make me leave my home."

Mr. Kim went to the front door and locked it, then shook it hard to make sure it was shut. Hector slowly moved to put a small bag of nuts into his pocket.

"What did you see out there?" Mr. Kim said.

"Like what?" Hector replied.

"Anything? People? Did you see people?"

"We saw some people on the bridge," Hector said.

"You seen anything else?"

"No, just people."

"The people, how'd they seem to you?"

"I didn't see any sign of the disease, if that's what you mean," Antoine said.

"I seen some sick people two days ago," Mr. Kim said. "Very bad... They will die soon. Very bad."

"What disease?" Hector asked.

"*What disease?*" Mr. Kim repeated back. "Where you been? Locked up somewhere? What disease? The thing that's been killing everyone."

Hector put a peanut in his mouth and chewed slowly, taking in the new information.

The store owner said to Antoine, "You a vet?"

"Yeah, and what the fuck's wrong with that?"

"Nothing, nothing. You fight a lot over there?"

"I did my share."

"Then you seen *them* up close. And you fight *them* and live," Mr. Kim said.

"Yeah, I've fought 'em."

Mr. Kim nodded and put the gun into his pocket.

"And just *who* are you two talking about?" Hector asked.

"The evil! The men who are not men. They walk our streets like standing shadows. They come from another world to kill us all! They are here now. I've seen them myself. Unnatural. They bring the disease, and now they come to check if we are dead."

Hector whispered under his breath, "Él está loco."

"Go turn off the lights!" Mr. Kim said. "You don't want what's out there to know we're in here."

"Then maybe you should turn off your sign," Antoine said.

"My sign is on?"

"That's how we knew this place still had power."

Mr. Kim said. "Then turn it off! The switch for the sign is the one underneath."

"How come you have power?" Antoine shouted from behind a wall. "The whole city is dark."

"I have a generator in the basement." Mr. Kim said.

Outside the front window, the dust that should have settled remained floating in the air. The night seemed misty gray and eerie and quiet like the hush of snowfall. The dust was caking on everything. The truck had a nice healthy pile on it.

"You can stay the night and have something to eat. Eat the fruit. It will all go bad soon anyway," Mr. Kim said. "You should wear dust masks. They're in aisle three."

And put his own back over his face.

The four of them sat on the floor in the open area between the registers and the front window. They watched the dust come down and ate in near darkness by the dim light of a single votive candle placed in the middle of them. Hector slipped potato chips under his mask and sipped on chocolate milk through a straw. Antoine took off his mask and threw it to the floor. Hector reluctantly removed his, but adjusted the one on sleeping Adrian.

"Is he sick?" Mr. Kim asked.

"No," Hector said, "just tired."

"You sure."

"Yes, I'm sure."

"What are you then? His nurse?" he said with a smirk.

"I'm his friend."

Mr. Kim stared at Hector for a few moments. "What is with you people?"

"What people?"

"Why do you feel the need to be like that?"

"It's none of your damn business," Hector said.

"Humph."

"*Pendejo.*"

"And you," Mr. Kim said to Antoine. "When you get back?"

"Recently," Antoine said.

"Was it bad over there?"

"It was bad."

"But this bad?"

"Yeah."

"Yeah?"

Antoine stood up and went to the window. The streets were encased in darkness. Something moved in the shadows. Maybe it was a person. Maybe it was something else. It didn't seem human, though it walked on two legs. But it wasn't an animal either. It strode with an elegant gait. Long tall strides. Upon its head was something like a hat made out of piping that stretched high into the air like a crown.

"What you looking at?" Mr. Kim asked.

"There's something across the street," Antoine said.

"Get away from the window."

Mr. Kim blew out the candle and they were doused in complete darkness. Only the waning moon shifting through the dust clouds provided any light.

"Gimme the gun," Antoine said.

"No, it's my gun."

"Which one of us knows how to really use it?"

They stared at each other for a long, tense moment. Then Mr. Kim looked down.

"It has no bullets. I only use it to scare people."

Antoine bent down and whispered, "Where do you keep the bullets?"

"In a box behind the counter."

Antoine took the man's gun and crawled to the counter, behind the cigarettes and candy bars and packets of gum. He groped around searching for a box.

"They're on the bottom shelf," the man whispered from across the room.

The shifting metal shook like maracas against the cardboard. Every tiny *snipk* of a bullet entering the gun reverberated in the hush.

"Stay down," Antoine whispered. He approached the glass, the gun silhouetted against the moonlight that filtered through. He stood unmoving, waiting. Then he angled his head and put the gun in the pocket of his coat.

"It looks like whatever it was is gone," Antoine said as he returned to sit down.

"Are you sure?" Adrian said to everyone's surprise.

"There's nothing out there now. Don't worry, bro. I got you."

```
>> recover

*RECENTLY DELETED FILES RECOVERED*

>> run diagnostics
>>
      .

      .

      .
```

The cold linoleum floor was hard on my back. Hector tried his best to make me a bed out of stuff from around the floor. I watched him as if seeing his body move from the other side of a thick glass. All the edges were fuzzy, and no matter how much I wanted to, I couldn't focus. I knew he cared for me. I just didn't remember why.

The smoke settled. The sky returned to its usual shade of blue. The day was bright. But the people were gone, and it didn't look like they were coming back. Antoine spent most of his time looking out the window. He said he saw something the other night. If he said so, he probably did. The others wonder and worry what it was. As for me, I was trying to get my bearings straight. My head still didn't feel like it belonged to me. And it was clear that I needed a shave.

I searched the store for where they kept the razors. I found them not in an aisle, but behind the counter near the disposable cameras and cigarettes. I took several packages of the ones with five blades and went to the bathroom. There was no running water, so I had to do it the hard way.

I left the door wide open and set a burning votive candle on the edge of the sink. Before me in the mirror was a ghostly, haunted man. Dark shadows lay under my eyes, and my beard had gown long enough that it was curling at the ends. I looked like Zeus or maybe a Caesar. I began to dry scrape at the hairs on my face. The razors got clogged so I had to start a new one over and over and over again. The heavy hair came off in clumps. When I finally got close to the skin it was a tricky business. The first nick stung like a mother. I used a bit of toilet paper to patch the wound. Then I nicked myself again and again and again. Soon my whole lower jaw was covered by tiny Japanese flags.

```
>>

*DIAGNOSTICS COMPLETE*

==> ERRORS FOUND: FRAGMENTATION IN MULTIPLE FILES
==> ERRORS FOUND: FRAGMENTATION IN MULTIPLE SECTORS
==> ERRORS FOUND: FRAGMENTATION IN KERNEL
```

RUNNING REPAIRS

.

.

.

Adrian was beginning to feel a bit more like himself again.

"Hey, good looking!" Hector said. "But you're supposed to use toilet paper on the other end."

"Ha, ha," Adrian said. "You're real funny."

"I do my best," Hector said, smiling. "You feeling better?"

"Yeah, I feel much better...thanks to you."

"It's no problem, Papi. That's what you do when people aren't feeling well. You take care of them."

"Thank you, Helen."

Hector soaked in the name like perfume.

"No, Papi, thank *you*."

Adrian tugged at the edges of the patches on his face. One by one he peeled them off. The brown blood stuck them to his skin for tiny moments until they gave way. He tossed them into the sink, where they drifted into the basin and collected with the scraped hair bristles at the bottom. They looked like tiny flower petals on a bed of freshly cut hay.

The night was cool. Clouds rolled by, casting moon shadows on the buildings across the street. Antoine insisted on everyone staying indoors at all times. He knew something, and he didn't want to say what it was. Adrian wanted him to share, if only so that he wouldn't be bearing the knowledge alone. Adrian didn't know what to say to him, or how to ask. He watched him staring out the window. They barely spoke. It got so that Adrian couldn't stand it. Antoine warmed up a bowl of instant noodles with water he boiled in the coffee maker and brought it over to him. Antoine looked at his brother with red-rimmed eyes. He said thank you as he accepted the cup. And they sat together watching the dark shadows roll by.

Then Adrian saw it. He turned to his brother. Antoine had his finger to his lips to tell him to hush. It moved like an animal. It had a strange stride. Adrian had to stare for a long time to accept what he was seeing. It stood on two legs and walked like a man. But its head was not a man's. At first it seemed like a hat. Adrian squinted. The darkness was thick and the dust was still falling, so he felt like he may have been mistaken, but the creature seemed to have antlers.

Bang! Bang! Bang!

Someone pounded on the window. Adrian jumped back. His heart pounded as if it would leap out of his shirt. "Come on! I know you're in there. I can see you. Let me in!"

Antoine had the gun pointed at the glass. Adrian watched his brother move.

"What do you want?" Antoine said.

"Don't leave me out here! Please let me in!"

Antoine faced the shadow. He stared at the dark figure for a long time.

"Whoever you are, leave us alone."

"You can't leave me out here! Dammit, they're coming!"

"What's coming?!" Hector yelled.

"Oh, God," Antoine gasped and backed away. "Everyone grab something! That broom, something heavy. Anything you can hit with!"

"What's going on?" Hector said.

The shadow man left the window and ran swiftly down the street followed soon after by a pack of other shadows. The sounds of hooves pounded the pavement, shaking the floor and making the windows tremble. Some of the shadows stopped and began banging on the pane. There was no time. It broke open like the crash of a wave against the rocks.

Shattered glass flew everywhere. Hector used his body to cover Adrian. A large shard slipped into the neck of Mr. Kim. He dropped to the floor and gulped for air as the blood gushed out of him. Antoine pulled Hector and Adrian to their feet and yanked them into the back storage room and locked the door behind them. The things thumped mercilessly against the door. Adrian and Hector pushed hard to block their entry. Antoine tried the back exit. It was heavy and locked. He shot around the knob several times until a big hole opened, then pushed the door into the alley. Antoine and Adrian ran out, but Hector slammed the door shut behind them, using his body to keep it closed.

"What are you doing?!" Adrian said.

"Run! I'll keep them here for as long as I can!" Hector shouted.

"You can't do anything! Get out of there! Come on!" Antoine screamed and pulled at Adrian's shirt, dragging him away.

Adrian cried, "Helen, why?!"

If he had remained for a moment longer, he would have heard the answer, "Because you saw the real me."

.

.

.

REPAIRS COMPLETE

9.

Adrian and Antoine ran until their lungs burned. Adrian's side ached with pain. He stopped to catch his breath.

BREAK

```
>>
>> opendoc /w process_data.fi

# process_data.fi -- update data,
# from hierarchical tree, sort
# and process data
   .
   .
   .

    parent = pop(hierarchy_data);
    child_1 = parent->left;
    child_2 = parent->right;
   .
   .
   .
>>
>> execute process_data
```

Two brown boys chased by fast-moving shadows and something-like-hounds. The galloping hooves drove them onward. They raced into an empty lot. Old soda cans, trash.

Broken glass, everywhere.
People pissing in the stairs like they just don't care...

Red bricks that used to be a part of a building stood one on top of another. You could almost make out how the rooms were once laid out. Antoine knew this area well. He had been here many times with his friends for his nighttime sneak-outs to do God knows what *'til the break of dawn*. Adrian had always helped him to creep back into the house. Their Dad never knew. If he had, he would have killed them both. In exchange for his silence, Adrian got the stories. The stories of who did what, when, and how. The stories of the music and the rhyme and the rhythms and the beats. He did this every night, every night, every night, repeat.

Antoine pulled at him when Adrian slowed. A beat. *And you don't stop.* They passed the graffiti practice walls on crumbling buildings designated for demolition with official letters from the city plastered on their doors. No one came to this place anymore. So the kids used the walls to work on their art. On the sides of these broken brick buildings were bold splashes of color. The smell of paint still lingered in the air. Empty spray cans littered the grounds among the other trash that Antoine and Adrian ran through.

They headed for the foundation of an abandoned apartment building that still stood erect. Adrian followed Antoine as he scrambled down into the basement. Antoine held a part of a boarded-up window open. Adrian didn't want to go inside. The fear made him crawl down fast.

> *Don't push me cause I'm close to the eeeedge,*
> *I'm try-in' not to lose my head...*

Their bodies were small enough to slip through. Antoine could still get on the bus for a ten-year-old's price even though he was fourteen. Adrian would be twelve and a half in the fall.

They landed in the dark. Adrian was breathing hard. Antoine put his hand over his mouth to make him quiet. The thing that was following them growled by the window and paced back and forth, sniffing. Antoine stretched his neck to look behind them through a small hole in the wooden board. The animal was made of flesh and metal. Its green eyes glowed. The silhouette of its master was tall against the moon, with antlers that spiraled up like twisting metal pipes. The thing heard its master's call. After a time, it padded away. The sounds of its feet grew distant, then silent. Antoine took his hand off his brother's mouth and Adrian drew in a deep swallow of air because he had been holding his breath.

"Where are we?" Adrian asked.

"Shh. Don't worry," Antoine whispered.

"It smells like piss," Adrian whispered back.

"I know."

"Can we go home now?"

"No."

"Why not?"

"I told you why before."

"Maybe Dad got better..."

Antoine didn't say anything for a long time. He walked into the light that shined through the large hole in the roof. Adrian went up to his big brother and gently pulled his jacket sleeve.

"Dad'll get better, won't he?"

Antoine looked down. A beat. "I don't think so."

Adrian knew that it was probably true. He didn't want to believe it. Everyone that got the disease went strange—grown-ups and children, too. The dust changed people. The disease made them sick. Over the past few days they had seen people change. Folks with scales running up and down their necks gulping for air like fish. Monkeymen with bowed legs swinging from lampposts. The dust was changing their dad. If they were lucky, only his body would change. If they weren't, he'd catch the disease and he would be crazy, too. It would make him do things that he didn't mean. He might hurt them. Antoine didn't want to take a chance, so he ran, taking his little brother with him.

Adrian began to cry.

"Don't worry, Adrian. I got you. You're my *boy*. I'm gonna take care of you now. I won't let anything hurt you."

They left that basement and walked uptown in the dimness of daybreak. The streets were a deserted mess. Cars stopped in traffic with no one in them. Newspapers and trash flying around. Smashed windows on the storefronts. And silence. Their footfalls echoed off the tall buildings. Behind the gray clouds it was speckly, like a monitor screen gone wrong. A small green dot hovered up there. Adrian watched it for a while as they walked until it blipped out of existence.

Whenever they heard something or saw something move, they hid. Abandoned storefronts, an old wreck of a house, and alleyways all made good hiding places. Something moved. It could have been anything. It could even have been someone who was still normal. Antoine wasn't taking any chances with Adrian's life. So they took cover and waited for whatever it was to pass.

Things fell apart so fast. Who would have guessed that the city could look this way so soon after the incident? That's what their dad called it, the Incident. He seemed pained even saying that much. Now their dad was gone. But Adrian had Antoine. He was going to look out for him. He would always look out for him.

The sound of feet came from behind them. Antoine pulled Adrian into the entryway of an office building. They quietly went inside, climbed the stairs, and went to the second floor window to look down. Two men were strolling by. They walked with bowed legs. One of them had something in his mouth. The tail and the squeal suggested that it was a rat. The dust did this, and maybe the dust would do more.

They looked carefully before they went back to the street. Antoine walked as though he had no fear. Adrian had enough fear for both of them.

They came to a subway station and went down to the platform. Antoine jumped onto the track. The trains didn't run anymore.

"C'mon," Antoine said.

"I don't wanna go down there," Adrian said.

"It's the only safe place right now. No one knows about it but me."

Adrian still didn't move.

A cold wind blew from deep inside the tunnel, carrying a nasty smell. Adrian turned his face away. He didn't like enclosed places, especially dark ones. Plus mounds of garbage mired over the tracks from way down into the darkness of the tunnel, and he thought he saw something moving in there.

"Adrian, I said come on!" Antoine said. "We can't stay here. The only place safe from the dust is underground."

"I don't want to go in there."

"I've been here a million times. It's fine. It's a secret place. Don't you wanna see?"

Antoine was always talking about the special secret places he knew about that he would show Adrian when he got older. Finally being in on his secrets was what moved Adrian's feet. Antoine took his hand and helped him down onto the track.

> Death creeps through the streets over programmed
> beats. A rabid dog in heat on a dead end street. Oil
> slicks: the only rainbows canvas gray concrete.
> Shadows of skyscrapers fall when Mohammed speaks.

> Corpses piled in heaps. Sores and decay. Reeks.
> Placin tags on feet. A Nike Air Force fleet. Custom
> Made: unique. Still in box: white sheet. Ripened
> Blue black sweet. White tank top, wife beat BREAK.

> Hearts in two-step beat BREAK.
> Dance pray work whip beat BREAK.
> Neck back jump back kiss BREAK.

> Now shake it off.

Their eyes soon adjusted to the darkness. They walked over the gravel that lined the area next to the train tracks. Strips of daylight slipped in from the underside of a grate above. The light illuminated the wall they walked past covered in graffiti, the bubble words so high passengers on trains would be able to see them. Antoine pointed out a small area where the words swirled to a round red dot surrounded by glowing white highlights. In it was a scribbling of black magic marker writing. Adrian couldn't read it.

"That's my tag," he said.

"Yeah?"

"I wouldn't tag something like that now. I didn't know any better back then. I hope the guys that did this don't catch me."

Adrian laughed. He could see his brother's eyes smile behind the shadows. A beat. The guys who did this were probably dead.

Adrian had always watched his brother work. Antoine sketched in his drawing pad, using magic markers to fill in the colors. The smell of the markers in his room was intoxicating.

Cool beats and rhymes from MCs blasted as he drew curvy lines that stretched and twisted over and under and through. *Spelling names, naming places, placing times, timing rhythms.* Adrian begged and begged his dad for a sketchpad, too. When he got it, he did as Antoine did, only different. When he sketched, he drew faces. Faces of the guys down the way. Faces of the street lady with the shopping cart and the bags of cans. But the best work he would ever do was the memorials.

Memorials would spring up on the sides of shopping centers, on the walls of the playground, by the barbershops. They seemed to appear overnight, and no one ever knew whose work it was. They'd spelled R.I.P. in large elegant curvaceous lines for the many brothers who had passed on before their time. Some from bullets, some for other reasons. No one ever tagged them. They would stay up for years. Someone obviously cared for them, refreshing the paint. Adrian had made two of his own by now. One for a kid he barely knew from school, who hadn't had a beef with anyone, but got shot for being in the wrong place at the wrong time. One for his friend Steven who died of cancer in the summer of last year. Now that everyone was gone, Adrian felt lost. There were too many faces to remember. There weren't enough walls to paint them all.

Antoine took him deep into the tunnel. He stopped at a metal door and opened it. He turned on the light. It was a maintenance office. Inside, there was a room with a toilet and another with a desk and papers all around. In the corner was a small couch, and beside it was Antoine's stash—a box full of spray cans. Adrian picked up one with a red cap. It was heavy with paint and made a *clack-clack-clack* sound when he shook it.

"We can stay here for a while," Antoine said. "No one comes here anymore. We get power from the solar panel outside. So we won't be in the dark. Move underground. Always gotta go underground."

Adrian sat down on the couch. The weight of his feet was heavy. So tired.

"You bring your sketch pad?" Antoine asked.

"Yeah."

"Good, me too," he said. "You got anything new?"

A beat. He did have something that Antoine hadn't seen yet.

"Yeah, I've been working on something but it's not done."

"Can I see?"

"Not yet."

Antoine smiled. "That's cool. Now you're thinking like an artist. Don't never show your shit before it's ready."

"Did you bring any food with you?"

"A little. That store had a lot of stuff in it. I should've taken more."

"Yeah, me too."

"I think I'll go back there and get more stuff."

"But those things are out there."

"I know, but we haveta eat."

Adrian looked away. Everything was so bad. And their dad wasn't around to make things right anymore. Not like after their mom died. BREAK.

"I don't want you to go."

"I'll be back soon. Don't worry," Antoine said and flashed that smile of his. "They can't catch me, *son*! I got this!"

The smile was infectious.

"Okay," Adrian said and Antoine left him alone and, for the moment, safe.

```
** BREAK **
>>
>> .
>> createdoc check_for_daemon.fi

# check_daemon.fi -- check if daemon process
# is running in the background

ps -ef | grep -v grep | grep Gauns

# if not found - equals to 1
if [ $? -eq 0 ]
then echo "Found daemon process..."
.eof
```

```
>> execute check_for_daemon
>>
.
.
.
```

Antoine left two days ago and hadn't been back since. Adrian waited in the cold maintenance office, too scared to move. The things were out there. Maybe they were in the tunnels. Maybe they were waiting for him out on the streets. It didn't matter. Antoine was gone. And he probably wasn't coming back. BREAK.

As his stomach twisted with hunger pains, Adrian sketched. Magic markers squeaked and scratched over the paper. The rhythm of his hand made music on the page. He drew face after face after face. Over and over and over again he drew. Strange faces. Faces of friends. Faces of the fellahs from around the way. Faces of the kids at school. Different faces. He stopped and looked over all of the pages he had done. The faces had merged into one. They were his brother.

Antoine. Antoine. Antoine. BREAK.

There had been a hum in the tunnel that was now silent, and the lights began to flicker. Had Adrian understood what that meant, he would have left the room then. It meant that power was no longer going to the pumps that kept the groundwater out of the tunnels. It meant that the underground was about to flood. The silence soon became unbearable, so Adrian opened the door. Water was flowing almost up to the steps of the office.

He packed his sketchbook and as many spray cans he could carry and walked out into the tunnel, stepping carefully through the dirty water. The further Adrian walked, the more flooded the tunnel became. He walked until the water reached his waist, holding his bag over his head. Wet and miserable, he climbed the stairs to the street. Adrian was afraid of running into one of those things. But he was hungry, and he wanted to find his brother. So he wandered down the long avenues of the city, listening to his feet scrape the ground.

In his heavy knapsack he carried the several cans of spray paint that made up the colors of his essential palette: red, green, gold, brown, black, several cans of white, yellow and a small can of blue. The remaining cans he left in the box hidden behind the couch in the maintenance office. He thought he could get them later. He pictured them underwater now.

He searched all of the places he knew Antoine liked to go—the old harbor that overlooked the next state, the cement park where the skateboarders used to hang out and practice their moves, the park in the square where the green market had met three times a week. All of them empty—no Antoine, no anyone. Only the lonely howl of the wind and the sounds of birds flapping overhead. And it was cold.

The sky above remained gray, the blue never returned. The dust had settled and formed an even layer on the ground. Adrian ventured out during the day and spent his nights huddled in the small corners of high-rise offices, his knapsack of spray cans for a pillow. Once, when passing the city hall, he saw an elk. It was wandering between the parked cars, then striding along the sidewalk puffing white cold smoke. It stopped for a moment and the two stared each other. The moment passed, and it made a slight sound like the whinny of a horse. For a moment, Adrian thought it was trying to speak. But then the elk turned its head and walked away, disappearing down the long corridors of the streets.

Adrian found canned stuff left in abandoned shops that was still good. He felt loneliest when he ate. Mealtime was when he and his father and his mom and Antoine used to talk. Mostly Antoine, though. Antoine would tell jokes that he'd heard, or dreams that he'd had the night before, or stuff that had happened that day in school. Now meals echoed the silence of the crunch or the swallow and nothing more. BREAK. Adrian didn't understand when his dad said, "Adrian, you could rule the world if you put your mind to it, but Junior… I don't know about him sometimes." How could he not know that Antoine was the center of the universe? Adrian could see it. He could plainly see it.

Adrian painted on walls. The once forbidden places now belonged to him. He chose the cement side of a government building first. He worked all day. First he laid out the outline in white, checking his sketch pad to make sure he got the proportions right. His fingers were covered in gloves with the tips cut off, and his face was masked so he wouldn't breathe in the paint fumes. By nightfall, his mural neared completion. His brother's large face stared back at him. He put the finishing touches on it before he lost the light. A light spray here, a little highlight there, and the metallic finish he wanted on the letters was complete. Instead of R.I.P., he put only a name: Antoine. That's when it hit him. The only way Antoine would be away this long was if his brother was never coming back. Adrian crawled into a ball and spent the night sleeping next to the mural he created. It was a stupid thing to do with those things still roaming the streets. But it was the closest he'd ever be to his brother again.

He painted another memorial on another wall. And another and another. He decided that his brother would not be forgotten. Antoine's image would live on forever and ever. One time he gave his brother that sly smile that he remembered so well. Another time, his brother looked down, serious and considerate. It became a mission to paint his brother's face everywhere there was a blank wall. What else was there to live for? He went back to his old neighborhood—an empty ghost town of whispered memories. He painted on the wall of his old apartment building. This was where Adrian intended to create his greatest work: Antoine set in the night sky, floating as if living amongst the stars and above him an eagle with wings outstretched, hovering as if carrying Antoine into the heavens.

Something made a sound behind him.
>>
** BREAK **

Found daemon process...
>>
>>

He lingered over his finishing touches on the mural. He didn't want to leave it. *Stupid.* He slung his knapsack over his head and ran. They were close behind him. Almost upon him. A voice from above said, "I got you, son." Adrian felt his feet leave the ground as he was taken into the sky. The sun blocked Adrian's eyes. He saw spots and lines of blinding light. Strong arms closed around him, wings outstretched. Feathers flutter flutter against the static gray sky. He looked up into the face of his father, changed but it was him.

"I've been looking everywhere for you," he said.

And he flew his remaining son safely up with no mention of his namesake.

.

```
>>
>>
** INTERRUPT **

ERROR: SYSTEM FRAGMENTATION
ERROR: SOME DATA LOSS

** SYSTEM RESET **
```

.

.

.

10.

They started as little nubs burrowing out of her back. At first they itched like tiny insect fingers crawling up and down just under her shoulder blades. She tried to ignore them. Then she tried to hide them. Even the thick sweater with the holes in it couldn't cover the growing bumps. Adrianne didn't say anything to her father. He so desperately wanted her to be normal. She didn't know how to tell him that it was happening to her, too. He was so busy worrying about finding their next meal that he didn't seem to notice her strange behavior. There was a sweet pain in knowing that she was becoming like him. She wasn't sure that he'd see it like that.

Whenever her father flew away he told her how much he hated to leave her alone. Adrianne always knew he was not leaving just to look for food; he was leaving to look for people. He still believed that there were folks holed up somewhere down there—survivors—folks like them with their minds still intact. He wanted to find them and maybe form a community, maybe even rebuild a little of what once was. Adrianne had doubts that she kept to herself. She watched him open his wings high on the morning breeze and coast into the purple sky, ascending and flapping.

Flutter, flutter.

He had been gone for almost three days. She tried not to worry. It was hard when he was away that long. The mist was thick again. She hoped he could see his way home. He was probably in one of the bombed-out buildings, waiting until the heat of the sun burned off the fog. But he'd come back. He always came back....

Home was a high-rise office building. It was a shell of its former self, a metal skeleton. Broken glass was everywhere. Papers and the insides of computers were strewn all over the floors. They had cleaned it up when they arrived and made themselves as comfortable as possible. Adrianne used one of the offices for her room. She liked having a door. It meant privacy. She needed that, or so she thought. She spent her days reading and writing in a journal, a leather-bound fancy thing that she had found in the office supply closet.

A pigeon cooed and landed on the ledge outside her broken window. It poked its head in and jauntily hopped across the metal frame. It flapped its wings and took to the air. She watched it, a gray dot against the purple sky. She had a fire going in a small metal wastepaper basket. It kept her a bit warm against the cold. Her father had showed her how to make it without burning the whole building down. She stoked it with rubbish found around the office: memos, contracts, order forms, and other nonsense. Sometimes she read the memos to such and such about some-thing or another complaint or redress or whatever. They wrote that stuff like it was so important. She'd crumple it up, throw it on the fire, and watch it curl up, brown, and blacken to ash.

She remembered how on a night like this her mom once told her a story from "back home" as she tucked her into bed. Her eyes wide and fingers stretched for emphasis—

> Pitney jumped at sounds she heard
> and peered from wall to wall
> to see the ghost who should appear
> from out the entry hall
>
> Grinning teeth stained red with blood
> Pitney was sure she'd seen
> yellow and long and sharp they were
> from out the darkness gleamed
>
> Thunder clapped and lightning struck
> shaking the window frame
> she dived beneath the sheets and hid
> before the monster came

Pitney watched the sun rise up
But no duppies came to call
So what caused her this night of fright?
Grannie's stewpeas 'twas all

By the end, they both were giggling uncontrollably with her mother tickling her belly while telling her it was time to sleep. Now those days were gone. She had the story, but not her mom. And the story wasn't funny anymore.

At least she knew that nothing was in the building with her except the pigeons. They'd strung empty cans on computer cables along all the stairways. They'd make a hell of a racket if something were to cross them. In the early days, all their time was spent "fortifying the barricades." Office furniture and mostly anything they could carry barred the entryways to their floor. If anything got through, her father said he could carry her in his arms and fly away. And if he wasn't here, she was to go up to the roof and fire the flare gun. He'd come get her. He promised that wherever he was, he'd come get her. Seemed like a dubious plan, but Adrianne hadn't argued. She knew he meant what he said. He was doing the best he could.

Her father returned, coasting with his long wings and circling as he made his descent through the window of their floor. Adrianne folded herself into his arms and stayed there, not wanting to let go as he patted her head and said, "I told you I'd come back. I'll always come back for you, baby. I'll always come back...." She treasured the sound of his voice—every utterance, every word, every syllable.

He was barefoot and looked a bit bruised. Adrianne noticed that he'd lost more of his facial hair. His face seemed extra smooth. He'd stopped shaving a while ago because his beard had stopped growing. Now the hair on his head was going, going, almost gone. And something about his bone structure had changed, too. More of his jawline could be seen, and his head was longer, more stretched out.

He pulled from her arms and said, "I've got a surprise for you." He drew out of his pocket a tiny, tiny kitten so small that it fit into the palm of her hand. Its eyes were filled with terror, but it stretched out its neck when she scratched it with her finger. It folded itself into her arms and was so exhausted that it fell asleep.

He unwrapped a blanket filled with food he had brought back. He had all kinds of stuff—cans of soup, crackers, peanut butter— enough to keep them going for weeks. He'd even found a live chicken somewhere. He'd cracked its neck and brought it along. Adrianne felt queasy watching him pull off its feathers. It seemed like preparing to eat a distant cousin or something. But they needed protein. It was gonna die out there anyway.

They had a feast that night. The smell of cooking warmed Adrianne from the inside. After dinner, her father felt so good he launched into telling stories about the ol' days when he went to clubs uptown and wore his fine clothes. Then he hummed an old tune while Adrianne kept rhythm by clapping hands. He got up and danced without a care in the world. Adrianne couldn't help laughing. It was a good time. Their bellies were full and the cat was curled up asleep by the fire. They were safe and they were together.

The cans from far below in the building rattled. A loud cry from outside. They had forgotten themselves. Her dad quickly doused the fire and Adrianne grabbed the kitten. They went into the furthest corner of the office and huddled in the dark as the sounds outside grew louder and louder. Her daddy's wings covered them like a shield. Slowly the howls became distant and faded away.

Early the next day Adrianne watched her father fly into the thick mist. He was going out to look for survivors again. He didn't say it, but Adrianne knew that was what he was going to do. It was as if he admitted that it was people he was looking for instead of food, he would be admitting that they were most likely all alone. And her father refused to accept that. He needed to believe that people could survive and still be sane out there, living life like them. He didn't want to raise Adrianne in a world devoid of life. So far all he had found were things that he didn't want to talk about. Adrianne had long ago given up believing that there was anyone else left. If there were people out there they would have found signs of them already, or so she thought. She kept her doubts to herself. They held each other close before he said good-bye. He reminded her about the flare gun and that she should go to the roof and fire it if there was any trouble. He would come right away, he said, and she believed him. Or, at least, she tried to believe him.

Her mom hadn't been affected by the mist. Neither had Adrianne—until now. But her daddy was different. He had started to change right after the dust fell. After days of him bent over screaming and sweating, small feathers began to sprout from his back. Her mom had tried to hold him, had wiped his forehand with a cloth. It was all she could do. She told Adrianne it was a sign—a miracle— her daddy was becoming like an angel. Adrianne knew her daddy was no angel. Angels didn't have wings, cherubim did. Adrianne learned that in Sunday school, but she didn't bother to correct her mom. Believing Daddy was touched by God seemed to help her. His wings had started out small and then grew and grew. Now they were so big he could wrap them around her and then some. She liked the feeling of them against her skin. They were so soft and light.

One of those crazies had gotten to her mom one night when she went out looking for supplies. She came back with bite marks on her arm. They thought she would be okay since it was the mist that was dangerous. But within days blue veins were winding through her light brown skin. The scales came in next and kept growing until they covered her all of her neck and worked their way to her face. They covered her arms, too. She would make a funny *gluck-gluck* sound between sentences like she was trying to swallow or catch her breath. After a while she got a crazed look in her eyes like the others. Daddy had had to fight hard to keep her under control.

One night it got so bad, her father told Adrianne to go to her room and to not come out no matter what she heard. The next morning her mother was gone. He told her that her mom had died in the night. He didn't look her in the eyes for weeks after that. Adrianne knew what he'd done. She didn't blame him, though. He loved her mom. He loved her too much to let her be like that.

*

The nubs pushed and pulled and squeezed past her shoulder blades in the night. She sweated with pain as the nubs emerged through her skin. She twisted and turned and screamed. It was so cold, now that winter had finally come. She could see smoke clouds steaming out her mouth as she threw off her sweater and the thin arms covered with feathers painfully stretched out of her back. Her dad wanted her to be normal. How could she let him see that the mist had worked its magic on her, too? The orange morning warmed her cold sweat, and her wings were fully outside of her body. The feathers were light and the color of ivory. She stretched them to their full expanse. They had started out so small. It took only a few hours for them to grow as wide as she was tall.

She didn't greet her Dad when he got home. She hid in her room with only the kitten to keep her company. A knock on her door. He didn't wait for her to say come in. He just did. His wings brushed against the door frame. They were not like hers. They were bigger, and his feathers were gray with speckles of black splashed everywhere. He held her metal bowl with dinner in it. He sat down next to her without saying a word. He handed her the bowl and folded his legs and looked off into the distance.

A big broken window in her room faced the city, so they could watch the darkness fall as the sun went down. By squinting, Adrianne could almost pretend that the city was still alive and that there were people in the buildings—working late and calling for Chinese food, or packing up and getting ready to go home, or getting dressed for a night out. You know, living and doing what folks used to do in the city. The illusion faded and reality slipped through. Those were broken buildings out there. Lights came on because some automatic generators were still working. That wouldn't last for much longer. The city was an empty urban shadow. A ghost.

Her bowl was warm and smelled good. There was some rice and beans in it and a spicy sauce her dad was good at making. She tepidly spooned some into her mouth. The gravy was salty-sweet against her tongue. She felt every grain of rice. She closed her eyes and absorbed herself in the moment.

"So they came in, huh?" he said. Adrianne winced. The food in her mouth turned to mush. She didn't want to eat any more. He put his arm around her and kissed her on the forehead.

"No need to be ashamed, baby," he whispered. "It just means you take after your ol' man."

This made Adrianne smile, though a tear rolled down her cheek before she could catch it.

"Why is this happening?" she asked. "Why are we changing like this?"

He sat in the quiet for a while as he thought how to answer.

"I think somewhere out there someone touched a button that they shouldn't a' touched. I don't know who and I don't know where, but that's what I think happened."

"Why would someone do something like that?"

"Baby," he said and sighed deep, "There are people that just don't care. They do what they want, when they want. Other folks just don't figure into their equations."

He swallowed and leaned in and put his head on hers. She put down her bowl and found a place under his chin to rest her forehead. She could smell his smell. It was her Daddy's smell. A sweet musky scent that filled her nose and made her feel safe.

"Before all this, my biggest problem was finding a job," he said. "I looked and looked and there was always someone more qualified. Someone with more education. Someone better. I beat those streets like they had done something to me to find work. A black man never stood a chance in this city. They fixed it so that we always got a raw deal. Then all of this happened and none of that mattered anymore. Now all I want to do is protect you." He kissed her tenderly on the forehead again.

"I want you to have a future," he said wiping away the flow from his nose and eyes. "All I want is for you to be all right. And these here wings, that's just what happened. Maybe they'll be the only thing that'll happen to you. And that's alright. I've seen things out there, baby girl…people twisted into all kinds of shapes…"

He touched her on the head and said, "I'm sorry for the world I'm leaving you…. You gotta be strong now, gotta be stronger than strong."

He got quiet. She wanted to ask about what he had seen. She wanted to know what more might happen to her body and what more had happened to his. She knew he didn't have the answers, so she said nothing.

"Tomorrow I'll take you with me on a food run," he said to her surprise.

"Really?"

"Yeah, really. You got wings now. You might as well learn how to use 'em. I'll teach you and then you'll come with me."

She swallowed.

"But Daddy, what if I can't fly? Mine might not work as good as yours."

"There's only one way to find out now, isn't there?" he said.

She touched her dad's hand, and then he said, "You should eat your dinner before it gets cold."

11.

Adrianne followed her father down the stairwell and through the barricades to the fourth floor. She hadn't been down there since they'd moved into the building. The floor was empty, with only a few unadorned columns to fill the vacancy. The glass from the windows had mostly fallen out, like in the rest of the building, so that the wind flowed freely through, almost as if they were outside. And yet, even with its vacantness, there was something less lonely about the fourth floor. Since no one had ever lived or worked on it, it was as if nothing bad had happened there. It seemed only unfinished, still waiting for the workmen to come.

Her father stood by a window and stretched out his wings. He waved them back and forth, then up and down. Adrianne, awed by his wondrously surreal beauty, remained still—watching. He motioned for Adrianne to join him. She stepped up to the window frame and stretched open her wings. Hers weren't as wide as his. But she did as he did, waving her wings back and forth, then up and down.

"Flying isn't flying exactly," he said. "It's coasting. You have to catch the wind in such a way to let the air lift you. It's a trick. Follow me and do as I do. I won't let you fall."

Adrianne *was* worried, though. She'd seen him fly many times. He had to know what he was talking about, she thought. He jumped out the window. Her eyes followed him as he swooped and coasted. An eternity seemed to pass before he returned to the window and gestured for her to come while fluttering his wings. She glanced at the street below and her stomach sank.

"Don't look down," he said. "Just dive out. Don't worry. I gotcha."

Adrianne, with her eyelids shut so tight that all she saw was hazy red darkness, jumped. The wind rushed against her face and body as if she were on an out-of-control carnival ride. Her arms swung violently, waving like crazy. Her eyes opened, and her heart panicked as the ground grew nearer.

"Stretch out your wings and feel the air!" she heard her father shout.

The pavement was closing in when the strong arms of her father grabbed and pulled her up.

"Feel the air!" he said, in a not very calm way.

Her thin third and fourth arms shakily stretched out. She felt a sudden lift as the wind gathered beneath her wings and picked her up like a giant spatula. The air became hard and real as if it were a solid thing like her father's arms. Adrianne went higher and higher. Her dad had let her loose long ago. She was flying.

"Good, good. Now you're getting the hang of it," he cried. "See, that wasn't so hard." He smiled and waved his wings.

Her father darted away. Adrianne followed. The wind dragged at her wings, making it difficult to control her direction and speed. Her father lingered for short moments as she struggled to catch up. When she drew near, he flew on—forcing her to fly harder and to be stronger. It was working. With every moment there was an increase in her coordination until she too was coasting, side by side with her dad.

They soared together above the large main street that divided the caverns of the midtown in two. Adrianne had not seen this much of the city in a long time. Broken glass, smashed-up buildings, and overturned cars crowding the streets and sidewalks. Blackened scars from the intense out-of-control fires that had burned themselves out, charcoal-marked the streets and sidewalks. In the silence and stillness, only the birds moved among the ruins, unharmed by the mist. The remains of several military drones lay crushed and broken on the ground. Adrianne remembered watching them shooting at the crazies and hitting normals instead, back in the days when they thought the disease had a military solution. Now, her dad guided her to a roof where they could set down. She stood next to him, the whole city spread out before them. The river beyond was black against the purple-gray sky, and smoke floated off the water. Adrianne felt a sudden chill.

"Every time I come out here I'm amazed at how messed up the world is. It will never be the same again," he said. It was hard to tell what he meant by that. He didn't exactly seem sad while saying it. He put his arm around her shoulder and asked, "How ya doing, Adrianne?"

"I'm okay, dad," she said.

"I wanna show you how to shop for food," he said. "There are lots of supermarkets and bodegas with good stuff still left in 'em. In the early days, after the change, most of them were stripped bare, but some still have stuff if you know how to look."

He climbed to the edge of the roof and dove off. Adrianne held her breath, stopped herself from looking down, and jumped too. This time with her eyes open, staring ahead as she sailed in midair with a sick elevator-drop feeling in her stomach. She flapped her thin back arms once in a while to remind herself that it was her wings keeping her aloft.

They maneuvered through the city caverns, between buildings, stopping to rest occasionally on rooftops that her dad knew well. Skimming over the river thrilled her. Seeing all that flowing water without anything to obstruct her view made Adrianne feel powerful, exuberant.

The neighborhood where her dad led her had many two-level buildings that remained somewhat intact. In places nature had taken over, miniature forests where broken townhouses had given way to the weight of decay. Her father pointed at moving things. Five or six of them. The trees interrupted the view. There they were again, awkward and bow-legged—used-to-be-humans—crazies, throwing rocks at Adrianne and her father.

"Happens every time I come here. Just stay high out of their range and you'll be fine."

They swooped over the borough. They flew towards an old storefront with windows and door smashed in that looked pretty picked over. They landed anyway. Her dad was a very smart man. He knew that the shelves would be empty. But they always forget the basement, he said. He forced the front door open with his shoulder, and they went inside. They found the door to the basement in the back. The steps down led to a nasty-smelling room mostly filled with empty boxes and dead rats. Her dad kicked around at the boxes until one of them made a thud. Gold mine: a box of canned Vienna sausages! He picked up a can.

"Always look to see if it's bloated or not. If it looks like it's getting ready to burst, toss it, 'cause it's no good. These, on the other hand, are just fine," he said. The white of his smile shined even in the dark. Her mouth watered just thinking about the soup they were going to make with the new ingredient. They grabbed a few plastic shopping bags from an open box and put all the cans they could carry in them.

Upstairs there was a crash, the sound of moving feet. Adrianne and her father stayed quiet in the basement for what felt like a long time, until it sounded like whatever was up there was gone. Her father climbed the stairs, and she followed. All was quiet and still but for the few birds that pecked on the floor, mechanically nodding their heads.

Outside, Adrianne and her dad found men who weren't men waiting for them. Bowlegged, twitching and jerking, they had scales all up and down their necks and faces and were swatting at invisible flies.

Her dad moved in front of her before she could do anything. Adrianne had never seen him fight before. He scratched and punched and threw bricks and rocks. Adrianne was horrified and also mesmerized watching a father fight to defend his child. Adrianne threw one of the cans she was carrying and hit one of the used-to-be-men square on the shoulders. She was aiming for its head. She threw another can and another and another. He father grabbed her from behind and pulled her aloft. A gust caught under her wings and lifted her as she threw another can. When one of the things grabbed at her ankles, she dumped all the cans left on its head. Her dad pulled her up high, and they watched the creatures pick up their treasure.

After that, her father decided that Adrianne wasn't ready to go with him after all. He said she was still too young. He left again to look for survivors, leaving Adrianne behind. What he was searching for might not be out there.

It had been over a month and still no daddy. He was never away this long. The mist was back, too. It choked the sky. Adrianne had set off the flare gun on the roof, and still he hadn't returned. She had always been afraid to think of the day he didn't come back. Now the day had come. Adrianne was alone.

Adrianne heard noises in the night. A large crowd of something passed by the building. She couldn't see what they were because the mist was so thick. Her flare might have caught the wrong kind of attention. All she could do was hide in the deepest corner with her kitten, her wings covering them like a blanket.

Adrianne decided to look for her dad. She pictured him hurt, moaning in some darkened alley in need of help. He would never approve, but he was not around to stop her. She had wings. She could fly. And she could be strong, too. Stronger than strong.

She put together a carrier bundle with food, water, and a few small things to help her on her search. She also made a special secure pocket in her bundle for carrying the cat. The feel of his warmth, the soft patter of his heartbeat, his gentle occasional purrs made her feel less alone. He let her pick him up and place him into his pocket, making only the slightest *murr*. He was more docile than he should be. She noticed that whenever she stared into the kitty's green eyes and saw more than a cat. The mist had done its work on him, too.

The bundle stretched over her neck and tied at the waist so it didn't get in the way of her wings. She looked at herself in a cracked mirror in their makeshift living room. The frame was made of plastic, and some of the mirrored coating had rubbed off. The image it returned was not to be trusted, yet she looked in it sometimes, marveling at the changes in her body. Adrianne hadn't looked in it since the wings came in. She was too afraid of what she might see. Her eyebrows were now gone and her hairline had receded. Her face was brown and shiny, her head elongated. Her hand glided over her head. It was porcelain smooth. She was a strange kind of beautiful.

One final check on the kitty. He slept snugly in his pocket, lightly purring. Adrianne was glad he wasn't fussing around in there. She closed her eyes to mentally prepare herself for the flight.

Then she leaped.

The wind blew her off balance, making her flounder for a few terrifying moments. Spinning, confused, disoriented. Her father wasn't around to help. Adrianne had to help herself. She straightened out and glided for a while. After a time she felt ready for her journey.

They floated over the great park that had become wild. The inhabitants of the zoo had gotten loose and were roaming around. A herd of elks ran free. Behind them were two cougars, charging at the slowest and weakest. It was hard to tell how much of this was normal. Some things were affected by the mist while others were not. She wished there was someone to ask why. Maybe the man who had pushed the button knew, if he was still alive.

Adrianne banked and flew toward the river by way of the bridge. It was still a grand affair, Gothic and sturdy against the purple-gray sky. The piled-up rusting remains of the cars formed a design of twisted metal along its span. The cat poked his head out just enough to catch a breeze on his nose.

She darted over buildings until she reached the neighborhood her father had showed her before. There was nothing, not even a hint of the creatures that had attacked them before. She spied another busted-out bodega and circled a few times to make sure it was safe before she landed. Memories of the fight she and her dad had the last time they landed here played in her mind. There was not much left inside, but she did find a few cans of cat food sitting on a shelf. She loaded a few in her bag and took to the sky as soon as possible.

She went deeper into the borough, flying over an unwieldy forest that used to be a green garden and saw things moving in the trees. Whatever they were, they were not human, not any-more. No sign of her daddy, though. She landed on the roof of the old museum to rest her wings. She remembered coming to this museum once when she was little. It was nice inside. A good memory of a time not so long ago. She sat above the frieze of statues etched into the stone. An impressive dome rose behind her. She opened a can of cat food and fed the kitty. He ate greedily, to Adrianne's pleasure.

She felt peaceful. The kitty, sated with his meal, curled up to sleep in his pouch. Adrianne was nearly asleep when a *click-click-click* sounded from behind her. She turned. A swarm of what looked like hundreds of large roaches, almost as big as her cat, were climbing up the stone walls and over the dome. She flew up into the air and didn't look back.

Crossing the river she spied something on the water, near a broken dock where the water was shallow and the grasses grew. It was a mass of large feathers, too big for a bird. And there was blood. She looked around and saw no other sign of her father. But this was him. She could *feel* it. Adrianne thought she was prepared. They had both known that this day might come. But nothing had prepared her for this. *Daddy?*

He was gone.

Their encampment in the office building was empty save for the memories of the man she'd loved most in the world. She let the cat out of his bundle. He shook his head vigorously, getting his bearings. She made a fire.

It was nighttime and all blackness. Only the light of the waning moon provided any light. Panes of glass from distant skyscrapers fell and broke against the ground, sounding like a leaky faucet dripping ice crystals. She made a little bed out of some old sheets and towels nestled into her daddy's old spot. It made her feel close to him. It still smelled of him. Then she lay down on her stomach to avoid crimping her wings, folding them back as best she could, but they somehow were always in the way. The cat curled up next to her and murred sweetly. He sensed how sad she was. Water flowed from her eyes uncontrollably until she fell asleep.

In her dreams she was herself but not herself. She went to the in-between space, neither here nor there, moving in and out of her body with ease, being herself then staring at herself from another's point of view. There was a rattling of cans. Something was in the building. *Daddy?* It was by the door. Adrianne edged toward the window. It was dark in the middle of the night and the mist was coming in thick. She wanted to flee but she also wanted to stay. A hope of her father's return stilled her feet.

She waited by the window, waited and waited. A blackness came through the door. The presence of it, the height and weight of it. It shuffled and moved with bow-legs. It had her daddy's face covered with scales and red, red bloodshot eyes. His beautiful wings were gone, or rather his feathers had been pulled out. His third and fourth arms writhed where they had once stretched wide to take flight. The man she knew was gone, replaced by a thing that walked in his skin. He came at her, eyes crazed and wild. He pushed over desks and chairs, reaching out for her. He bared his teeth, which were red with blood.

"Daddy?"

It only returned grunts. She knew what had to be done. He would have done it for her. Maybe that was why he had returned. Some part of him that was still her dad, wanted her to do for him what he did for her momma. At least that was what Adrianne made herself believe. Her hand shook as she pointed her flare gun. Every fiber of her body ached as she squeezed the trigger. The gun fired. He howled, waving his flaming arms. He still grabbed for her. Adrianne was too far away. She jumped backwards through the window and coasted into the rising mist...and woke to the sound of rattling cans.

Quietly, Adrianne gathered her cat into his pouch. He was fully awake and could sense the danger and moved deep into his bundle. His scared green eyes stared into the darkness. He fussed only a little as she dove out the window. From a distance Adrianne could see through the skeleton of her building, now infested with a multitude of the creatures. There was nothing more she could do. *You have to be strong. You have to be stronger than strong.* She comforted her cat and flapped her wings and flew north.

```
>>
>>
>> bridge status

connecting...

*BRIDGE RUNNING WITHIN NORMAL PARAMETERS*
*OBJECTIVE AT 0.564853556485 OF COMPLETION*

==> ERRORS IN MULTIPLE SECTORS
==> FRAGMENTATION
==> POSSIBLE DATA LOSS
==> ERRORS BYPASSED

*SYSTEM BRIDGE MAINTAINED*

>>
>>
>> continue

BRIDGE PROCESS: CONTINUED
     .

     .

     .
```

12.

A scrim of fog settled on the window, making the world outside appear in white silhouette. Weather was not the cause of this, though the winter's frost had finally come. It was the dust. The unbeatable dust that mixed with the water in the air and made the mist. It seeped underneath doorways, clothes, and skin. Changing people. Changing the world. Changing his wife. Adrian dared not listen as the doctor examined her. He stared through the cold glass pane with the cat who slept silently on the window seat, wishing that Netta and the baby were going to be all right.

The door to their bedroom squeaked open. The inside of Adrian's skull felt hot. The news, the news, the god-awful news. He didn't want to know. He needed to know. So that he could make the plans. He was always full of plans. That's why everyone turned to him. His plans fixed things. But there were no plans for this. There was no fixing this. Nothing to fix. Nothing to do. Nothing. Only a plain simple truth: his wife's body was failing, and she was taking their unborn son with her.

Dr. Thomas came through the door, wiping his hands on a towel. Adrian breathed deep and forced himself to face him.

"For now, Netta and the baby are stable," the doctor said. "But she should not be moved. Complete bed rest. That is my suggestion."

Adrian swallowed.

"Are you sure she wouldn't be safer out of the dust?"

"You are sealed in well enough here." The doctor pointed with his stethoscope. "Look, I know that many want you to move underground, but I am not interested in politics, only the health and well-being of my patients. My prescription is firm."

"I understand."

"I hope that you do," he said. "Her condition is very delicate. Moving her would most likely kill her and the baby."

The word "kill" did the job it was supposed to do.

"She won't be moved."

"See that she isn't," the doctor said.

Adrian cracked open the door and peeked into the bedroom. Netta dozed sweetly in the bed. Long plastic lines of fluids connected to drip tubes that connected to bags of liquid that connected to machines. The complex spider's web surrounded Netta, delivering to her frail, failing body life-sustaining medicines. She and the machines were becoming one. He carefully closed the door, leaving her to sleep undisturbed.

"I will come back in two days to check on her again."

"Thank you," Adrian said, more than sincere. He had to hold back from grabbing the man into his arms and weeping. Dr. Thomas was very busy with all the sick and dying. To take the time to personally come out and care for his wife was well beyond the call of duty.

He escorted the doctor to the door and watched him put on his head covering. It was a large scarf that wrapped around, folding over a flap that went atop his nose and mouth, leaving a small space for the eyes. It was the fashion these days for keeping the dust off the face and skin.

"See you soon," Adrian said.

"Two days," Dr. Thomas' voice echoed distantly from inside his wrap.

The plastic covering of the first door released pressure with a hiss and closed with a *swoomp*. Adrian watched as Dr. Thomas bounded through the short vestibule to the outer door, holding his doctor's case in a bio-bag.

Adrian returned to his bedroom, inched the door open, and saw that Netta was awake and gesturing for him to come in.

"Hey baby, how ya feeling?" he said, as if to a small child.

"You tell me. What did the doctor say?" There was real fear behind her red-rimmed eyes. "How is the baby?"

"You and the baby are fine. You just have to keep still. That's all."

Adrian crawled through the lines of fluid and curled up in the bed beside her. With the tip of his index finger, he traced along her jawline, down her neck to where layers of dried skin scaled, flaked, and were peeling off. A single drop climbed out the edge of her eye to stream to her hairline.

"Shh," Adrian said, wiping away the tear. "It's gonna be all right."

"Promise?"

"Promise."

Adrian leaned his head against hers and wished he were the woman lying in the bed. He held Netta in the quiet of the beeping machines. Time had no meaning then. They were all together, she and him and their unborn son.

"I had a dream last night," Adrian said.

"Yeah?" she said.

"It felt so real, like I was really there. I dreamt that my father was showing me how to fly and he had wings like an eagle." Adrian used his hand to show the swooping and sailing of flight, opening his fingers wide like feathers. "When I woke up I couldn't go back to sleep."

The door signal light flickered.

"That must be Sheila," Adrian said and untwisted himself from the cords and lines attached to his beloved and went to greet the nurse.

Sheila came through the vestibule with two men. Adrian waited as they resealed the plastic door covering and unraveled their various head and face wraps. Sheila's toothy grin brightened the room, and she stretched out her arms. The cat rubbed itself against her legs. She gently edged it away.

"It's cold outside today. Long time since it's been like this," she said. She took her things and the coats and wraps from the others and put them away in the closet. Her muffled voice murmured from inside, "I think I'll make you a nice stew for dinner."

"You don't have to do that," Adrian said.

"I want to," she said. "It'll be nice for a change. Now lemme go check on Netta while you talk with your people."

Sheila headed to the bedroom rubbing her arms as she went.

Kim patted Adrian on the shoulder and shook his hand, then gestured at the other man to guard the door.

"She's right. It *is* cold outside," Kim said. "What do you think that means about the air?"

"Don't know," Adrian said. "It could mean anything. But I don't think it means anything good."

The corners of Kim's mouth curled down.

"So how are you doing?"

"I'm fine," Adrian said, looking away.

"Are you moving down into the city?"

"The doctor still says I can't move Netta."

"Doesn't he understand the situation?"

"The situation doesn't matter. I'm not going anywhere until it's safe to move her."

"Okay, okay. I didn't mean to upset you."

Adrian nodded and wiped his face with the back of his arm. He took some moments to compose himself, and Kim gave him the space by looking away.

The clock ticked in the quiet. Finally, Kim handed Adrian a memory card. "These are the updated plans. All the changes you suggested have been implemented."

"Including the redirection of the lower ventilation shaft?"

"Yes."

Adrian inserted the memory card into his table computer and brought up the plans. The wide smooth glass of the table displayed the detailed line drawings of every inch of the city being built below ground. Adrian traced the lines with his finger, checking.

"This looks good," Adrian said. "I did a redesign of the second-level air pumps last night that should increase their efficiency another six percent." He pulled up his new design and laid it over the table. Kim leaned in to see what he had done.

"This just came to you in the night, huh?" Kim said.

"I had a dream and then this came to me," Adrian said, still staring at his plans. "It should work."

"Knowing you, it will more than just work," Kim replied. "A security detail is downstairs waiting for you."

"Expecting any trouble?"

"Word has gotten out about the city. Stragglers are showing up trying to get in. Nothing we can't handle."

"I want security here."

"Already done. Don't worry. She's safe," Kim said. "And I'm staying to make sure."

The closed bedroom door loomed large in the corner.

Adrian said, "All I do is worry."

A faint smell of burnt ash drifted on the wind. It itched at Adrian's skin. He removed his headwrap to readjust it to cover more of his face. Cold smoke rose out of his mouth as he re-wrapped his head with the scarf. When he looked up he noticed a small gathering of men. They stood against a ragged skyline made hazy and faint by the mist. Some held large machine guns strapped over their shoulders. Others held them slack, pointing down. They all wore black headwraps and red bandanas that hid their faces. Adrian hadn't been expecting this show of force. One of the men pulled down his face wrap and approached him.

"Remember me?" he said.

Adrian considered him from a distance. There was something familiar about the mole over his left eyebrow and the shape of his chin.

"We didn't exactly run with the same crowd. But I remember you. You were one of those smart-ass kids, always playing chess and what not."

Slowly Adrian remembered his name and reputation. He was called Jolly. His smile with that underlying hint of menace told of the kind of humor he had. Even when they were little he was a developing gangbanger. Adrian had stayed far away from kids like him in the old neighborhood. What the hell was he doing here?

"Yeah, yeah. I can see you know me," Jolly smiled. "All that old stuff is water under the bridge now. Me and my crew got your back, man. You and your ol' lady upstairs." He held his gun like he knew what he was doing. "My daughter's in that city you're building."

Adrian looked over at the men holding the guns and wondered if these were the same knuckleheads who used to spend all their afternoons on the street corner back home, do-ing god knows what. Strangely, it did make Adrian feel bet-ter to know that they were the ones protecting him and his wife. They were all survivors here; everyone was under the same threat of annihilation. Like Jolly said, that old stuff was water under the bridge. Circumstances change everything. They began their walk through the broken city. All was quiet but for the echoing sounds of their feet scraping against loose gravel and cracked pavement. The men walked behind, nervously scanning the areas around them and pointing their guns every which way. Adrian looked up at the tall building that was his home and sighed deep within his chest. The park where they were going was only a short distance away. That was one of the reasons why he and Netta had bought the condo. They'd had visions of walking with their someday-children to play on the grass on Saturday afternoons. They never envisioned this wasteland. Who could?

As they approached, he could feel the digging machines working in the distant part of the park. The pounding of the earth beneath their feet shook the few remaining trees. A crowd was lined up near the left gate. Men with guns stood by keeping order. Adrian knew that trouble was coming. The underground city was designed for only a certain number of people. Eventually folks would be turned away.

They went past the checkpoint into the center of the park and walked along a path that crossed over what used to be a baseball diamond. To their right a rustle of bushes and trees caused their guns to cock in unison.

"Hold up, hold up," Jolly said, and lifted his gun to his shoulder as an elk bounded off into the distance.

"What the hell is *that* doing here?" one of the men said.

"The zoo," Jolly said. "Some of the animals got loose when the construction started. They won't hurt anything."

The men went a little further down the path, over a walkbridge and down to a lower driveway to a well-hidden tunnel. Very few knew of this entrance. One of the men banged on the metal door three times, paused, then banged three more times. A catch released and the door opened. Hector, accompanied by more men, all with machine guns, greeted them.

"Hey, Adrian," Hector said and waved them inside. "Everyone is in the conference room already."

Down, down, down in the elevator open on one side, save for a waist-high gate. The smell of dirt and hot steel deepened as they descended. The gated door opened to loud construction. Where they stood would be black as pitch but for the radiance from bright spotlights shining further down in the construction pit. Adrian followed Hector through a construction safety corridor to a door restricted to official personnel only. Adrian pulled his identification card out of his pocket and swiped it through. His number appeared in red on the screen: one-seven-seven. They entered a hallway that became perfectly quiet once the large metal door shut behind them.

In the conference room ten people sat around a large table. Four men wore suits and ties. Two women sat extremely close, deep in conversation. One had red hair and freckles and was rifling through some papers. One was Stephen, a really good engineer. One had gray eyes and never had much to say. One was the head of the group, Dionne Maiter, a no-nonsense woman in steel-rimmed glasses. Adrian and Hector were the last to take their seats.

"Let's get started," Maiter said. "How is the construction coming?"

One of the suits answered, "We are approximately thirty-four percent behind schedule, and the lower levels are still incomplete."

Maiter said, "We can't afford to be this behind."

"It's a water problem," Stephen said and pushed his glasses back. "We're building beneath the water table and are still developing the pumping system. It's difficult for the crews to work on the city's construction while constantly battling the water."

"And we have a communication problem as well. The routers are blocked, and the crews can't work together when they can't talk to each other. Perhaps we should begin using the satellites again," Hector said.

"The satellites won't help us this far underground," Stephen said. "What we need is to make sure all the signal routers are in place, which they're not."

"Why aren't they?" Maiter asked.

"It's the pace of the construction. Every time we install the routers, the structures around them change."

"Maybe we can make mobile routing units," Adrian said. "It's foolish at this point to have them remain stationary."

Stephen nodded.

"As for the water problem, I've redesigned some of the pumping systems in my latest drafts of the construction plans to divert the groundwater into internal cisterns until it can properly be piped out to the river. It will help a little, but we can only do so much."

"Okay, then," Maiter said. "And, Stephen, I'll put you and your team in charge of developing the mobile router units."

Stephen nodded again.

"As for the satellites, I have to confess something," Adrian said. "I have been using them to communicate with my counterparts in other cities for months now."

"Why would you do something like that?" Maiter slapped the table. "The satellites may be monitored. *They* may find out about the underground cities."

"I doubt *they* care what we do," Adrian said. "They released the dust and haven't been back since."

"It doesn't mean they won't come back," Maiter said.

"They don't need to. They think we're done for."

Silence.

"Is that true?" Maiter asked.

"Maybe," Adrian answered.

The word "maybe" rang in the air like a tinkling cymbal.

"Eventually the dust will choke us all," Adrian said.

Stephen pushed back his glasses. "I think these aliens—these creatures who attacked us—knew exactly what they were doing. They've probably done this before to other unsuspecting planets like ours."

Adrian continued, "The cities are only temporary shelter from the inevitable."

"So then what do you propose?" Maiter leaned back, tossing her pen down on the table.

"I propose we leave," Adrian responded.

"Leave? Leave where?" Maiter asked.

"Leave Earth," Adrian said. Maiter actually laughed, until Adrian put a memory card on the table. Its click on the polished wood echoed in the silence.

"Myself and designers in other cities have been working on a prototype based on a downed invader's craft."

"A prototype of what?"

"A ship. A spaceship. We should build several."

He slid the card across the table toward Maiter, who picked it up and examined it as though the information it held was readable by the naked eye. She entered the card into the table computer, and a three-dimensional image appeared, floating in the center of the room. It was the schematic of a craft shaped slightly like an avocado.

"You're serious about this?"

"Dead serious."

It was as if no one in the room wanted to breathe. Maiter stared at the floating figure for several long moments then said, "Say this even works. Where would we go?"

"We found a terrestrial planet in a system that we believe we could reach," Adrian said. "Though there are a few significant differences from Earth, for instance, it's tidally locked with its sun, but we believe our people could survive there. Also there are some interesting properties in its atmosphere that we could take advantage of technologically."

"Oh, this is crazy talk!" Maiter said and slammed her hand down on the table.

Adrian swallowed. "A year ago I would have agreed with you, but now we have no choice but to face the hard reality. The people of this world are dying. If we are to survive, we have to leave."

13.

The image of the ship still hung in the air, spinning on its own axis. It was sliced at the center to show the design of its inner quarters. Its pear shape was awkward and squat. It would have been funny if only the situation weren't so dire. The conference room was now empty except for Adrian and Hector. They remained in their chairs, not speaking. The silence broke when Hector stood and walked across the room.

"Well, that was intense," Hector said.

Adrian continued to stare at his spinning design.

Hector pulled out a chair and sat down next to Adrian. "Are you all right?" he said and touched Adrian's hand.

"Yeah."

"How is Annie?"

It irked Adrian when he called her that. People called her "Antoinette" or "Netta," but no one ever called her "Annie."

"She's fine," he lied and then corrected himself. "She's the same."

"I'm so very sorry," Hector said. "Adrian, I want you to know that if you need anything—and I mean *anything*—that I'm here for you." They had been friends for as long as Adrian could remember. There were times when he wondered, had things been different, where their relationship would have gone. He looked into Hector's sympathetic eyes and felt the warmth of his touch, then moved his hand away.

Adrian said, "I know."

Stephen returned to the meeting room.

"Good, Adrian, you're still here," he said. "I was hoping to catch you. Can I talk to you for a minute?"

"I was about to head down to the lower levels."

"It won't take long. It's important."

The high-ceilinged hallways in the administrative part of the city were walled in cinderblock painted a yellowish off-white. The tiled floors echoed their steps as they made their way to Stephen's office. At the end of the hall they passed a temporary observation window, constructed so that the new city being formed could be seen from a safe distance. Dots of light flickered in the open pit like stars in the night sky. Pillars of steel were being erected by construction crews and the sparks from their welding sprayed like tiny fireworks.

Stephen's office was cluttered with neat piles of papers, files, and books lying on every available flat surface. He pulled out a seat, lifted off a stack of papers, and searched around for another place to put them. After several seconds of fussing, he put them on another pile in the corner. The newly created pile leaned precariously but somehow remained upright. Stephen offered Adrian a seat and then cleared off space on his table computer, angling the surface towards them.

"So what is it that you want to see me about?" Adrian asked.

Stephen pushed back his glasses, sighed, then rubbed his hair in an attempt to make it flatten. His curls sprung back unchanged. "We've been examining the dust, trying to understand how to reverse its effects in the atmosphere."

Adrian nodded.

"Well, we haven't learned much about the dust. Actually, we don't have the slightest idea how it works yet or how to get rid of it. It will probably take us years to understand, much less do anything about it."

Adrian nodded again somberly.

"But we have figured out something."

Adrian leaned back. "Yes?"

Stephen opened a window in his table screen and entered a few commands. A display of the spinning Earth appeared with a simulation of clouds floating like pulled cotton across its surface. Stephen entered a few more commands, and about twenty to twenty-five colored lines appeared crisscrossing the globe.

"What's this?" Adrian asked.

"Atmospheric encoding." Stephen rubbed his finger over the screen to maneuver the image and then zoomed in to show a closer view of the lines that divided the atmospheric layers of the earth.

Stephen smiled. "It's a method of etching a basic operating system into the earth's atmosphere. It would be powered by the sun and invisible to the naked eye."

"For what purpose?"

"There are a lot of ways we could go with this. We're still experimenting. We were kinda hoping that you might have some ideas." Stephen handed Adrian a memory card. "Here are the schematics for the system and our current methodology."

Adrian rubbed his developing beard. He had been forgetting to shave of late.

"For now, we are only uploading a message that's a warning to others about what these aliens have done to us. We set it to emit an intermittent signal so that if some intelligence comes along, they should be able to detect the program."

"Like the aliens who attacked us," Adrian said.

"Maybe—well, yes, they would be able to detect it. But like you said, I doubt they care."

Adrian stood and patted Stephen on the back. "It's a good idea, Stephen. Keep at it. Maybe there is something more we can do with it."

"But there's more...um...well, we are building a human interface program that will interact between the lower subsystems and the intelligence that may read the program. We want to use you as the template for the program."

"Me?"

"Yes, we all agreed that it should be you."

"Why me? Maiter is probably a better choice, she's the head of development—"

"A lot of people would be dead if it wasn't for you. You're the lead designer of this city. All of us on this project have agreed. I was voted to be the one to ask you personally if it was okay." Stephen pushed back his glasses and rubbed his hair.

Adrian leaned forward on the back of the chair, thinking.

"What would I have to do?"

"Just show up a couple of times in the lab for a few painless scans, and that's it."

"Painless scans, huh?"

"Guaranteed painless, like going for an MRI."

"Okay, fine. Just not right now. There are a few things that I have to do today."

"Whenever you're ready."

Adrian opened the door to leave and said without turning around, "Thank you for thinking of me."

Down in the lower levels, surrounded by heavy construction equipment, dirt, and steel, Adrian and all the men and women who made up the building crews worked at digging further and further into the earth, inserting supporting beams, carving the foundation for the new world in which their children would live. Day or night—in the blackness of these man-made caves there was no difference. For them, the movement of the sun was happening on another world.

Adrian could see so clearly what his city would look like, where the municipal building would be, the library, the schools, and a hospital. He was determined that this would be a place worthy of raising children. There would even be parks in this new world. The panels of artificial light he designed would flood this cavern with the warmth of the sun.

But he also wondered and worried as he watched his designs take physical shape. How would the city work? It would be up to the people to govern themselves. Could they? No matter how well he planned, he couldn't help with that.

He was lost in his thoughts when a voice screamed his name. It was Kim, standing on the other side of the pit. Over the banging, the hum and the crack and the sizzle of the welding sparks, he couldn't hear. Adrian edged closer to make out what Kim was screaming.

"Adrian, the baby's coming!"

"What?"

"The baby's coming!"

Adrian leaned in more. "What?"

"Hey, boss, look out!"

"Oh, shit!"

"Damn, is he okay?"

"Somebody get a doctor!"

"Don't move him!"

"Fuck, that's a lot of blood!"

"Where's the damn doctor?!"

"Fuck!"

"Adrian...Adrian...can you hear me?" The doctor waved his fingers before his eyes, then took some notes. "Reduce his dosage by 25 milligrams. Maybe tomorrow he'll be more responsive."

"Adrian...Adrian?" the doctor said.

Adrian moved his eyes toward him.

"Blink if you understand me."

He blinked.

"Do you know where you are? Blink once for yes, twice for no."

He blinked twice.

"You're in the clinic. We are taking good care of you. Don't worry, just rest."

The doctor tapped him on the arm and smiled grimly. Adrian felt feverish, as if he were smoldering behind his face. Heavy, drowsy. His head turned, his consciousness followed moments later. Cool lids closed over hot eyes. Slowly he drifted back to sleep.

The doctor peeled back the bandage on Adrian's head, exposing a stitched deep cut turning brown at the edges. Adrian submitted to his hand, staying still as the doctor placed a new bandage carefully over his healing hurt.

"And how is that back of yours?"

"Fine," Adrian lied.

"Let me check."

Adrian turned, lifted his shirt, and leaned against a chair. Large lines of unhealed flesh marked his back. The wounds appeared as if something were ripped off.

"Do you feel any pain?"

"Not really," Adrian said.

"Uh, huh. You know, there is really no use in lying to your doctor. It was a serious accident you were in. That scaffolding could have killed you."

"There are others who are in more pain than me."

"Maybe so, but the people need you to be clear-headed." Then the doctor remembered himself. "Or, at least as clear-headed as you can be."

He injected a medicine deep into the flesh near Adrian's spine. Within moments the pulsing pain of the wounds became numb.

"Thanks."

"No problem," the doctor replied.

Adrian pulled down his shirt.

"Doctor, I believe I'm well enough to see my wife now."

The doctor didn't answer, only put away his instruments and turned away.

"Maybe you should sit down."

"Sit down for what?"

"There is something that I need to tell you."

Cold blackness fell down like rain. Drenching clothes. Soaking them to the skin. Words, words, and more words. What was said made no sense. Sorry. We tried. There was nothing we could do. You have a son. Keep him. Raise him. She's not in pain anymore. Not one more day. Not one more hour. No more gasps for breath. No more suffering. She's not coming back. Was there sorrow? A whimper. A cry. A wail. Who made those sounds?

A snarl vibrated from behind the locked door. Adrian sounded like a large cat with teeth made for rending flesh. He hissed, then went quiet like a menacing dark spirit in the back of a cell.

"How long has he been like this?"

"All night."

A growl, low and intense.

"This is not working." The doctor wrote out a new script. "Stop the medication and give him this."

The window was a wash of nightfall colors. Orange drowned by pink and purple and blue, and a dot of green that briefly held in the air like a solid object, then faded away. A shadow bent his head towards the failing light. A man broken both in mind and spirit. His beard fully grown and curled at the edges, ungroomed and sprinkled with spit.

"Stephen," Adrian said, "I know you are there."

The little man stepped into the vanishing glow of the evening sun. No one else would come to witness this embodiment of grief. Only Stephen. He pushed back his glasses and rubbed his hair.

"You've been here for hours... almost every day."

"I didn't think you should be alone," Stephen said and drifted back towards the exit. "Don't worry. I'm leaving now."

"Stephen?"

"Yes?"

"Stay for a moment."

"Okay."

Silence.

"Have you seen my son?"

"Yes. Antoine. He is well. Sheila is taking care of him."

"Antoine? Good. That's good."

Silence.

"Have you ever thought about what will be left behind when we're gone?" Adrian asked.

"What do you mean?"

"What will be left of humanity? Ever wonder?"

"Sometimes," Stephen said.

"We are stripping our monuments clean so we can make our new underground cities. All our databases, all of the information about who and what we are, will corrode in a matter of years without human intervention. Our books will disintegrate.... There should be something left of us, don't you think?"

"I suppose so," Stephen said.

Adrian placed a memory card on the window sill.

"This is for you."

"What is it?"

"It's my plans for your atmospheric encoding project. Multiple layers of code in the atmosphere can be networked like a spider's web over the surface of the Earth. It should still run your warning program, but it should also be a giant database where we upload our books, history, all our knowledge.... It will be a memorial to mankind."

Stephen stepped forward and carefully picked up the card.

"Okay," Stephen said. "I can get started on this."

"And I want you to do something for me."

"Yes?"

"I want you to make sure that *she* is remembered.... I want you to make it so that the sky will have her memory living up there.... I want you to make her beautiful like she was...."

"I'll try."

The door creaked open, slicing a sliver of white into the shadow.

"Stephen?"

"Yes?"

"Thank you."

```
>>
>>

** PREPARING FOR DOWNLOAD **

enter access code:
enter access code:
* BREAK *

>>
>> continue

** ERROR: CANNOT COMPLY **

enter access code:
enter access code:
enter access code: Antoine
```

```
** UNRECOGNIZED CODE **

enter access code:
enter access code: Adrian

** UNRECOGNIZED CODE **

enter access code:
enter access code:
enter access code:
enter access code: 10110001

** PROGRAM DATA STREAM OPEN **

DOWNLOADING...

==> BRIDGE SOCKET 200983 OPENED
==> RECEIVING DATA STREAM


........x.....a........mf................
........................................
........................................
.......c................................
........................................
.......................q....3...........
........................................
........................................
......8.................................
........................................
........................................
.....................................1.....
........................................
........................................
.............r..........................
........................................
........................................
........................................
```

```
.......z.............................
.....................................
.....................b...............
.....................................
.....................................
.....................................
.....................................
...........×ì}K%9F:%²D…ii=ŽAôÖêKÄÏƒ¤
¥"'SŒ¥ækr¿Ï}©$ãÛ:³eP¢ö+¢_l½⊠<¡R¬¾q
™u,ùÑji‰S(=ÁuE¼Ë¨žTTO®ªù)ÊzAÐÖ¼&è°
>[ èvU~æ©»,¶à>b»g)=‡"«ù|Ò&Ýtú=u¸£*
Ð´¹!¥8Â'ŸíR>§€yÁÕkäó«*Ë7é¹6r)=‡"«ù
éU'&è°ê£¼°$@à\ªŸ-•|:Zl°Vwü¤üƒƒÇ<ë…
|Ó„4 É#'>ç\oä\œî>Œt¶Œ{üWõ®<ß•Ò©Au
lÃw4A;ÈnÁöÔ\9É9'åä$´™^..
```

```
** ERROR: SYSTEM OVERLOAD **

==> RECEIVED LARGE COMPRESSED DATA
==> ERROR: FRAGMENTATION
==> BRIDGE SOCKET 200983 CLOSED

** DOWNLOAD COMPLETE **

***********************************
** Please 'continue', there is   **
** still more to see...          **
***********************************


>>
>>
>> continue

BRIDGE PROCESS: CONTINUED
.
.
.
```

14.

The sky was a cloudless blue, blue, blue as far as the eyes could see. No sun, just blue. The fresh scent of ozone lingered in the clean air. The trees tempered the wind. The grass was soaked with dew. And the weather was warm, like it always was.

A bearded man sat on the park bench, wearing ragged shoes. Black dirt caked his face and clothes. His yellowing eyes gazed upon the children at play, running in a zigzag game of their own making, falling down to stain their clothes with green. Their laughter echoed high up into the firmament then back down. He smiled to himself and whispered words to someone who wasn't there. No one responded but he heard an answer.

Yes, this is good. This is very good.

He considered all the people with shadows under their eyes as he slowly rose. The creak of his legs made him feel old before his time. He clumsily hobbled across the soft lawn. The soles of his shoes flip-flopped—the rubber bands he used to keep them attached were lost or broken long ago. The soft grass tickled his feet. He laughed to himself with the sensation. Mothers pulled their children close as he passed, and some covered their kids' eyes. The bearded man was a harmless fixture in the park. Some even remembered who he was. Others didn't care and only wished he would go away.

He shuffled out of the park and into city streets thick with people. People, people, everywhere. All with the same sickened look and shadows under their eyes. They gave him a wide berth. It was the smell. He mumbled to a man who tried to give him money, "I made the sky, you know." The man nodded and hurried away.

Down the boulevard, he saw corner after street corner after street corner, on and on ad infinitum. He scratched his ass and smelled his fingers and laughed. It was all such a beautiful illusion.

He knew where he was going. Better than anyone, he knew the way. Past the stores and the vendors' tables that were lined up along the edges of the sidewalk with handmade crafts, T-shirts, scarves, and leather holders for the pocket gadgets. Past the shops and cafés. Past the people in their beautiful neat clothes and jewelry made of copper and gold. Their sounds were a blending stream of conversations and sighs. He stopped to stare at his reflection in the window of a clothing store, where the plastic people looked at the mannequins in their styled outfits. He didn't recognize himself, but it was him, only a him he wasn't sure he wanted to be.

The City Hall that he had designed himself was open to the public. He walked through the front door unhindered and shuffled over the tiled mosaic floors, taking a moment to stare up at the oculus, which drew in a large stream of light from above—the ceiling decorated so delicately with indented squares carved out to lessen the weight of the dome. He slipped into a back room and then through an open door to the outside into an alley, checking behind him to see if anyone followed. Of course, no one did. He stepped over the boxes and the bones from devoured fried chicken and through the potent stench of urine to touch a brick wall. He found the brick marked with a "T" in black magic marker and pushed at the third brick down. A door opened, and he walked through.

This was the place behind the walls, behind the sky, controlling the day and the night and the wind and—soon—the rain. The hidden place maintained by The Twelve, that everyone knew about but refused to remember. The secret rooms that Adrian had designed. He walked past the guards and the staff and all those who owed their very existence to him. He walked through the hall past the one-way observation window where the city was laid out to be seen. Through another hall, to the stairway made of cinderblock walls painted off-white. To the rooms above set aside only for him, where there was a warm bed and clean sheets and fresh towels. A home Adrian rarely came to because he'd rather sleep on his city streets.

He could feel Hector enter. The man who was his friend, but from a time long ago and a place of trying-to-forget.

"Honey...look at you..." Hector said, "you can't go on like this."

"Please, leave me alone."

"I'm your friend. I can't leave you like this... I know it hurts, but it's been years...."

"Leave me alone!" Adrian screamed. The words spewed forth like hot liquid.

"I will not leave you alone!"

"It's been too long. *She* would not want this for you. And what about your son?"

"That's why I'm here today. Today of all days. Today is a very important day."

"I know what day it is," Hector said.

"I'm back for my son. For my son. Yes, my son. My son and I are going to Elysium. We are going. Yes, we are going. My son and I are going. Elysium. Elysium."

"You shouldn't let Antoine see you this way. He still looks up to you... At least, the memory of you."

Adrian rubbed at his beard. Something came off on his hand, and he smelled it and turned his head.

"Yes, perhaps you're right."

"The bathroom is that way," Hector pointed. "And spend plenty of time in there. Scrub it all, honey, please. Scrub everywhere."

The shower stall was a clear glass-enclosed closet. Steam was his only curtain. Water spread over him like a cleansing rain. The warmth of it stimulated his limbs and soaked his skin. Shampoo with the scent of pear splashed into his eyes and stung. He scrubbed and scrubbed. Dry flaky skin turned into a darkened flow where it streamed towards the drain and gathered with the foamy remains of soap. Adrian was angry with Hector for invading his space, and he loved him for it. His presence outside the bathroom door made Adrian feel responsible somehow. Not better, just more responsible. He had to shave; someone was here. He had to eat; someone was watching. He had to clean up; someone could smell.

Adrian turned off the water and stood enshrouded in a steam so thick he could hardly breathe. Nothing held him, only the moist air. He was lost in time, surrounded by a warm humidity, a fog, a cloud, while thoughts of her buried and decomposing in the soil whirled in his mind. He hugged himself and rocked as if in prayer. Then leaned against the wet tile, moaning quietly.

"Hey, you all right in there?" Hector shouted from the other side of the door.

"I'm fine," Adrian said too quickly, with a flash of fear that Hector might come inside.

"You're so quiet... Okay, take your time. When you come out, I have a surprise for you."

Adrian lifted the toilet seat and let the warm pee stream out of him. He stared, mesmerized by his yellow creation. He flushed. His moist hand wiped the fogged mirror of the medicine cabinet. Facing back was him, and not him. He was somebody else. Someone he didn't recognize. Someone he didn't want to recognize.

"Papi?" The door opened and Hector's head came into view. "Oh, honey..." he said as he let himself in.

Before him was a ghostly, haunted-looking man. There were shadows under his eyes and Adrian's beard had gown long enough that it was curling at the ends. He looked like Zeus or maybe a Caesar.

"At least for one afternoon you're going to be your old self," Hector said.

"But I don't want to be him."

Hector put his arms around Adrian's shoulders. They stared at each other in the mirror. Neither was the person they used to be.

"Perhaps you should shave that thing off," Hector said.

"Perhaps I should."

Adrian searched the bathroom cabinets for razors and found them. He began to dry scrape at the hairs on his face. Each razor got clogged, so he'd start a new one over and over and over again. The heavy hair came off in clumps. When he finally got close to the skin, it was a tricky business. The first nick stung like a mother. He used a bit of toilet paper to patch the wound. Then he nicked himself again and again and again. Soon his whole lower jaw was covered by tiny Japanese flags.

"Hey, good looking!" Hector said when he returned to the bathroom. "But you're supposed to use toilet paper on the other end."

"Ha, ha," Adrian said. "You're real funny."

"I do my best," Hector said, smiling. "You feeling better?"

"Yeah, I feel better."

"Antoine is upstairs waiting for you."

"Yes?" Adrian said.

"Yes."

"I'm taking him to Elysium today."

"Yeah, I know."

Adrian tugged at the edges of the patches on his face. Then one by one he peeled them off. The brown blood stuck them to his skin for tiny moments until they gave way. He tossed them into the sink, where they drifted into the basin and collected with the scraped hair bristles at the bottom. They looked like little flower petals on a bed of freshly cut hay.

Adrian entered the room, freshly cleaned and somewhat sane. The eleven were there waiting for him. Four men dressed alike. They no longer wore suits and ties, only long-sleeved business shirts with the top buttons undone. Two women stood extremely close, like sisters. One had red hair and freckles and seemed nervous and out of place. Stephen the engineer pushed his glasses back and rubbed at his hair. Hector, his old friend, stood up smiling, happy to see him. The guy with the gray eyes looked at the floor and had nothing to say. Maiter seemed stern as usual, still in her steel-rimmed glasses.

"The people in the city look sickly," he said.

"The concentration of dust from the surface air has been increasing."

"I see. I thought that might happen." Adrian drew on a piece of paper. "Try this."

"What is it?"

"A new design for the scrubbers in the air filtration system."

"Okay," Maiter said, taking the paper. "We will look into this."

"The city needs to be bigger," Adrian said.

"We are digging as fast as we can."

"There's no space for the people."

"We've limited the birth rates to one-to-two a couple," Maiter said. "But it's difficult to keep up with immigration from above."

"Then stop taking in the sick."

"Dad!" a small voice said from behind.

Adrian turned around and saw his son. His little boy. Antoine. He took the boy into his arms and held him tight.

"I've missed you, Dad."

"Antoine," Adrian said, "I've missed you, too." He stared at his son. The very image of his mother. The same eyes and nose. The same curve of cheek. Beautiful.

"How old are you now?"

"I'm eight."

"Eight? Yes, that's right. Eight. You're becoming such a big boy," his father said. "And do you know what day today is?"

"Yes," the boy answered.

"What day is it?"

"It's my mother's birthday."

"And where are we going?"

"To the world above to visit her grave."

"Yes," Adrian said. "To Elysium. To the world above the sky."

Stephen stepped forward with a small device in his hand and said, "I'm going with you."

"Yes?" Adrian said.

"It's time to update the atmospheric encoding system."

"The Elysium system," Adrian said.

"Yes," Stephen said. "Elysium."

"I have the tribute file for Antoinette ready," Stephen said.

"Is she beautiful like she was?" Adrian asked.

"Yes, she is beautiful."

15.

Adrian and his son were with ten others in the elevator. A sadness lingered as they flew higher and higher, up to the surface. Flashes of light seeped through, periodically illuminating their somber faces as they passed the many levels of the underground city. The sound inside the shaft changed as the elevator reached the upper levels, becoming a long screeching sound like a wailing child. Then the elevator was immersed in the natural light that shined in from above.

Antoine leaned over to look out one of the windows in the door. They had reached the crust, the level between the very top of the city and the surface of the world. Stretching as far as his eyes could see were the great sheets of translucent metal used to produce the illusion of sky for the city below. They lay flat against the upper surface of the artificial world. Construction was still underway. One day they would undulate, to simulate the movement of the heavens so that clouds might appear and possibly even rain. Antoine could also see the inner workings of the atmospheric processors and the climate controllers that created the wind from the recycled air. No one but the administrators were allowed to see this level. No one from the city was allowed out into the real world anymore. The Twelve had ordered it so. And who would disagree? No one really wanted to see the mess that was made of it.

The elevator door opened on the surface level to a dark enclosed passageway. There was a hint of light from the other end of the hall. Everyone paused. No one said anything. Antoine was the first to leave the elevator. Then the others followed. The air felt hot and dry and still. They walked toward the light and stopped beside a short stairway that led to a door outlined by the glow of day.

The men put on black gloves and wrapped their faces with large black scarves. They were dark soldiers walking into the night like walking shadows. These men had a natural ability to fight the effects of the dust, still they knew they shouldn't stay on the surface for too long. Adrian helped Antoine, encircling his small head with a length of thick cloth.

"Can you see?" he asked Antoine.

Antoine nodded yes, then adjusted the cloth around his eyes.

One of the men produced a key card that glowed red on its edge. He slid the card into the slot next to the door. A heavy lock clicked. Then the metal door slowly rumbled open, allowing in the damp air.

They entered a world of grays. Gray drizzle fell on a gray horizon. Streaks of lightning lined the sky, and the roll of distant thunder shook Adrian's heart. Only a few buildings remained standing, and even they were crumbling, with great tree trunks growing into them, breaking the concrete and bricks. Rows of hollowed-out trunks lined the former streets with the wind howling through them, making them seem to speak. And everywhere the mist drifted like a living fog. Adrian looked westward, from what used to be midtown, to see the flowing black water of the river.

This was home. Elysium. A place of sorrow. A place of love. It was difficult to reconcile the two. In the silence, it was as if all that had ever existed in time and space was trapped and frozen here. Adrian didn't want his son to see this place. But it was where his mother lay, so it was where they must go.

A hulk wedged up from the old harbor, casting a dark shadow onto the landscape, a remnant of a time not so long ago. A little beyond it, out of the mist rose several avocado-shaped latticework constructions, the beginnings of his spaceships. Adrian pointed them out to his son.

"See that? Those are ships that will sail in space someday. When they are complete, I want you to go on one of them. It will take you to a better place."

Antoine stared, fascinated.

"I don't want you to spend the rest of your life buried alive in the bowels of the Earth. Antoine, you should go to the stars."

The group walked in the eerie quiet as if they were the only ones left alive in the whole world. In the night, anyone who remained on the surface would be hiding somewhere. Rumors said that things roamed the former streets that were best avoided.

"Stay sharp," Jolly whispered.

The guards soundlessly lifted their weapons and scanned the mist, searching for any movement, listening for sounds.

They approached the site of the grave. Upon it, a marble statue of a veiled woman looked down with maternal eyes. An oil lamp carved into her hand burned stone flames, and stalks of wheat and barley were etched at her feet. The marble image overshadowed everything. Its gaze went to far-off places. Brought here from gardens overseas, it was said that this statue had once been painted—sienna, burnt umber, olive, ochre. Its alabaster appearance came from years of exposure to the elements.

Antoine laid down on the grave a crayon picture of his mother that he made in school. He had only seen her in photos, so it was based on them. Her eyes were large with black irises surrounded in white, her skin carefully shaded in lines of tan. Adrian went to his knees and brushed away sticks and crisp, aged leaves with his bare hands. He whispered words that no one could hear and placed a kiss on his fingers, then put his fingers to the cold white stone.

The others waited uncomfortably in the mist. Stephen backed away and began to prepare the device for updating the atmospheric database. He removed a small rocket from the bag he carried. He set it upright on a welcome-mat-sized launching pad and ignited its engines. Within moments the small rocket *whooshed* into the air, higher and higher until it disappeared from sight.

"What da hell are ya *doing*?" Jolly said.

"I'm updating the atmospheric database," Stephen replied.

"No, you're tellin' every freak out here that we're here. What's fucking wrong with you?"

"Wha—" Stephen began to say when the rocket above burst into flame, flowering overhead into a multitude of directions, momentarily lighting the entire sky like a giant spider's web set ablaze.

"Fuck...me...." Jolly said.

No one else spoke in the moments that followed. Maybe it was the shock. Maybe it was the amazement. It was probably both.

The darkness returned. The silence returned. All was still.

"I'm so sorry," Stephen breathlessly said, rubbing his hair and straightening his glasses. "I don't understand. This never happened in the simulations I performed. This never—"

"Shh!" Jolly put his finger to his mouth.

A shift in the wind. A distant heartbeat. The sound of crashing trash cans. Something was out there. Something was coming.

"Everyone, let's move!" Jolly shouted.

"No," Adrian said. "I'm not ready."

"Then *get* ready. We gotta go!"

One of the guards picked up Antoine and bolted with the others. Adrian had no choice but to follow as they ran into the mist. Something was behind them. Many things, by the sounds of it.

Lungs burned. Hot breath parted the mist. Even with the fear, exhaustion set in after running so long. The things were behind them. Now they seemed before them, obscured by the thickened mist. The men pointed their guns into the fog.

"Easy. Shoot only on my mark," Jolly said. "They're probably just hungry folks out looking for some food. No need for bloodshed today. Just back away."

But the things didn't back away. They breathed in unison. Heartbeats. Voices low and guttural.

One of them stepped out of the fog. It walked like a man, but it was not a man. It had antlers that twisted up like a crown. Planar structures moved over its surface, flickering and sometimes cracking out of existence so that the eye could not quite capture what it was perceiving. The creature was more shadow than form, shifting and changing from moment to moment, making it seem multi-limbed and writhing through dimensional space. It stomped slowly toward the circle and pushed its head forward into Jolly's face.

"What da fuck are *you*?" Jolly whispered. "What do you want from us?"

The answer came like a fly buzzing in the ear. They all heard it. Words whispered close to the mind as if the wind spoke.

...hu-man...ver-min...die...soon...

"Fuck you!"

Bullets flew. The heat. The smoke. The smell. *Bdddbb, bdddd, bddddd! Bdddbb, bdddd, bddddd! Bdddbb, bdddd, bddddd!* Adrian ducked. The night was pitch black with repeating bursts of light. He moved to cover his son with his body.

"Antoine! Antoine!"

Antoine was gone.

A flash of green...

```
*** SYSTEM FAILURE ***


>>>>>>>>>>>>>>>>>>>>>>>>>>>>>>>>>>>>>>>>>>>>
>>>>>>>>>>>>>>>>>>>>>>>>>>>>>>>>>>>>>>>>>>>>
>>>>>>>>>>>>>>>>>>>>>>>>>>>>>>>>>>>>>>>>>>>>
>>>>>>>>>>>>>>>>>>>>>>>>>>>>>>>>>>>>>>>>>>>>

** BREAK **
>>
>> restart

BRIDGE PROCESS: RESTARTED

>>
>>
>> whois /current

Humans          12      0000-00-00 00:00
Roaches          8      0000-00-00 00:00

>> finger roaches

Name: roaches
Origin: unknown
Description:
An alien species called the Krestge
that entered Earth space and released
the dust that poisoned the atmosphere.



                .

                .

                .
```

They wore crimson cloth and copper-colored armor and mechanical wings that extended high off their backs and shined in the moonlight. Wings designed by Adrian so they could protect themselves in the land above, made of metal that they mined from deep within the earth. They had found this metal as they dug deeper and deeper to build the underground city. Metal he used to construct these wings so they could fly and cut.

Wings opened and slashed, slicing in every direction. Feathers of metal shot like knives, stabbing at alien flesh. The thick fog scrambled the senses. A blade grazed the skin of his arm. His wing flicked upward, slashing the creature in front of him. It gurgled and fell to the earth.

The others fighting alongside them—other humans who seemed to come from nowhere—wielded knives and sticks and other crude weapons. Several of the creatures flew up into the trees. The transparent skin between their limbs allowed them to take to the air like birds. Adrian and his men flew after them, cutting them down. The night filled with sounds of sliced flesh thudding against the earth. And then silence.

Adrian and the others raised their wings to beat back the mist so they could see. Many of those who had attacked them lay dead on the ground.

"Antoine! Antoine!"

"Dad!" Antoine came running into his arms.

Adrian held him tight.

Adrian fell to his knees to check the boy's condition. He moved his head from side to side, checked his neck and arms, turned him around to examine his back. He was fine. The child stood in the fog, curious and afraid.

Cloud smoke rose from their noses and mouths. The stench of rotting flesh, urine, blood, and feces reeked. The men adjusted their headwraps to shield their faces from the wind and the dust and the smell.

A dog with glowing green eyes clunk-clunked toward them, sniffing. Its front paws and part of its muzzle were made of metal.

"That's Roscoe. Don't worry, he's harmless if you're human," a pale man said as he walked out of the shadow, wiping blood off a large knife on his pant leg. "We got him from one of the roaches and retrained him." As he passed a fallen alien, he spat on it. "Fuckin' roach."

The haggard men emerged from the shadows, so ashen their skins seemed to glow through the dirt and blood that smeared them.

"I didn't know the aliens were still coming down to the surface," Jolly said.

"We've been seeing them walking around lately. Mostly at night. Roaches like the dark."

Adrian kicked at a fallen alien and turned it over. It was not what he had expected. It was bipedal and had an extra set of limbs. What seemed to be its face dislodged and rolled away. It was a face mask, probably to protect it from the effects of the dust. Its real face was thin and noseless and shadow. It had slits that maybe were its eyes.

"What brings you out on a night like this?" the pale man said.

"We were visiting a grave."

The pale ones laughed.

"If that ain't the dumbest reason I ever heard for risking your life. Dead is dead. Nobody gives a damn after you're gone."

"She was this child's mother. And we will remember her."

"Whatever."

The moon sat red and half in shadow on the horizon. It was big and thick as if one could reach up and pluck it directly out of the sky. Huge tree trunks lined the path, dead and hollow. They whistled as a breeze blew through them with a winter's chill.

"Thank you for helping us—"

"You're from the underground."

Silence.

"No use in denying it," the pale man said. "You look too healthy to be from the surface. Not to mention your metal gear." He reached out and touched Adrian's wing. "We want you to get us in."

Adrian looked at them closely.

"How many of you have the sickness?" Adrian said.

"All of us, even me." The pale man pulled down his scarf to expose a few scales running up and down his neck.

"I'm sorry then."

"You're going to take us to the underground."

"If you have the sickness you can't be admitted."

"Who are you to decide? Who the fuck do you think you are? Fuckin' filthy niggers! Who are you to tell us where we can go?"

And there it was. A memory of something Adrian had long forgotten. A class system that had died in the dust. Adrian looked around at his people and saw a truth that no one had spoken out loud. The dust had been discriminating. Those with more melanin had been spared its harshest effects. Their skin had protected them. It had protected him and it protected their son. He was so grateful that in this one way Antoine favored him. But soon, they too would succumb.

"You wanna say that again?" Jolly said, and the other guards arched their wings. The metal-on-metal feathers *shtyingged* as they rubbed against each other. The strangers edged closer and closer. Adrian moved Antoine behind him. In the silence were the sounds of heartbeats. *Thump, thump, thump.* Roaches. They could hear them. The roaches were coming.

"Run!" someone screamed.

And they all scattered. Some running here. Some running there. Some flying away.

Adrian extended his metal wings, grabbed his son, and soared with Antoine in his arms into the night.

16.

Sparks of fireflies flickered as the sky faded in shades of blue. It was the magic hour. The time when the sun sat on the belly of the earth and the light diffused, painting the surfaces of broken cement gold, pink, and terracotta. The air was still and soundless. The smallest movements made by even an ant seemed to be done with a hush. Adrian dared not shift the position of his wings. The ringing tones of the metal might wake his son, and it had taken him a long time to get the boy to sleep.

Maybe it had been foolish to take him to see his mother's grave. Maybe it was the selfish act of a grieving father. Adrian thought on these things while holding his son gently on a ledge in the crevice in the remains of a tall stone building. The smell on the air spoke of a coming storm. Later on it would rain. They must find shelter soon. For now, he would let Antoine sleep. His sweet, sweet boy.

As Adrian stretched out his wings, the metal feathers *shinged* like tiny bells caught in the breeze. The wind took them and they alighted to the air. Antoine opened his eyes.

"Are we going home now, Dad?"

"We will a bit later," his father said.

They soared into the clouds, descending occasionally to examine a spot below that seemed appealing. Rain began to fall. The drops of water sprinkled across his metal feathers and soaked his hair. Adrian did his best to cover his son while keeping the water out of his eyes. It was increasingly difficult to see, and his grip on Antoine felt like it was slipping, so he hurried to find a place to land.

Then he saw it. In all this time he had forgotten about the long stone building with its arched windows revealing cavernous insides. It was as magnificent as he remembered. He touched down on the broken red-brick plaza, and they walked to the stairs before its entrance. Four Corinthian columns stood like soldiers framing the doorway and towered overhead.

"Whoa," Antoine gasped. "What was this place?"

"A museum. A place of art," his father said.

Much of the ceiling was gone, and the building open to the harsh elements. The entry hall had holes overhead where rain came through, cascading down like waterfalls, sounding like a filling bathtub. He followed his son as the child excitedly explored. Antoine jumped over pools of water and touched the slippery marble information counter and the granite walls. Then he went to the center of the hall and spun and spun and spun in circles as he stared upwards at the once beautiful vaulted ceiling.

"Your mother and I used to come here before you were born."

"Mom." He stopped spinning.

"We would come here on Friday nights and listen to chamber music."

On a damp night almost like this one, Adrian had heard Chopin played here. It was his favorite of the Préludes that he had only known before from recordings, Op. 28, No. 15. The young man at the piano sounded out the rhythm of raindrops as if nothing around him mattered. As if the world outside had gone away and all that existed was the music. Each note rang high off the ceiling and hung like raindrops caught in midair. Time stood still, and Adrian was enraptured. He could hardly breathe. So beautiful. He closed his eyes as if to hear that piano again. He was woken from his memory by the warmth of Antoine's hand slipping into his.

"Dad," Antoine said, "you miss her, don't you?"

He smiled down at his son who was looking up at him with a tug of pain in his eyes.

"Every day," Adrian said.

He tightened his grip on his son's hand and said, "Let's go upstairs."

His metal wings *shing-shinged* as they climbed the grand stairway that led to the upper galleries. He folded them back to lessen the sound and their echo off the walls. They climbed hand in hand and carefully watched where they stepped for cracks and chips in the stairs. The glow of the moon coming through the open areas of the ceiling provided enough light to see by. His son tried to sound out some of the names on the large plaque of benefactors as they went.

They walked along the balcony that encircled and overlooked the entry hall. The glass cases along the balcony's walls that once held Asian ceramics were smashed open and empty. An archway to the left of the balcony led to the large exhibit halls that were no longer there. Instead, there was an open drop to the bottom floors. The building seemed as if it had been struck by something big and explosive to cause this kind of damage. But it was just time and nature doing their slow deconstruction.

Behind them were doorways to the galleries that once held the European paintings. The walls had been stripped bare in every room they entered. Adrian could picture the panic of the curators as they rushed to take down the paintings, secreting as many as they could to some storage facility while the madness outside raged. People knew they were going to die and were lashing out at everything. The fear was so thick you could smell it. Some people ran, but others took to the streets and slashed and destroyed.

It was left to people like Adrian to keep their heads. To strategize. To prepare. To make a way for the future. And to somehow preserve what they could of the past. Like the curators who took down these paintings. How scared they must have been—and how faithful. He wondered if they had made it. Maybe there was a place deep below them, protected from the elements and all the insanity that was the end of the world, where unbelievable treasures lay hidden.

Adrian closed his eyes for a moment and tried to remember what had been where. He wanted to describe the paintings to his son. But he couldn't remember. In the numerous times he had been here, the many instances he had wandered these very rooms, he couldn't recall what he had seen. So with a heavy chest, he said nothing. His son would never know the beauty that his father had once taken for granted.

"We should go down to the first floor," Adrian said. "There is something I want to show you, if it's still there."

They descended the grand stairway and went through the entry hall and to the right. There was a long hallway lined with Greek and Roman statues from the classical eras, some broken and smashed to the floor, others remained remarkably erect and untouched. Antoine walked around them, staring up at the men and women frozen in stone.

They turned a corner and entered a large open area with a side-wall made of glass like a large greenhouse. The panes were slanted on an angle all the way up to the high, high ceiling, letting in the cold moonlight. Many of the panes had fallen, so there were shards of glass on the floor on that side. Nature had taken over. Plants and trees were growing inside, and owls hooted above. This was the museum's replica of a temple built by the Romans for their subjects the Egyptians, complete with sandstone blocks and columns topped with carved leaves like a tropical tree. The temple grounds were surrounded by a stone moat that Adrian remembered being filled with clear, still water. He had once thrown a coin into it for good luck. Now it was a marshland of green and smelled of algae and slightly of sulfur.

Outside the glass wall was a forest where the mist had settled on the earth among the trees. Adrian's wings arched up—he thought he had seen something moving. Then a lonely elk stepped up to the glass and stared inside at Adrian and Antoine. It shook its head, its graceful antlers swayed, then it stepped back, disappearing into the cloud.

They crossed the small bridge that led over the marshy water to the temple replica. Both man and child touched the sandstone blocks, running their hands along the hieroglyphs and Roman letters etched into them. At the base were carvings of papyrus and lotus plants.

"We can stay here for the rest of the night," Adrian said. "I've always wanted to sleep in this room."

Adrian unharnessed his wings and let them gently fall to the floor. They *shinged*, then slapped onto the stone. The ringing of the metal feathers echoed. An owl looked down from above, hooted, and turned its head. Adrian cleared a spot on the stone floor and beckoned his son to join him. Antoine sat down, and they both leaned their backs against the sandstone. Adrian opened the small pouch he had attached to his waist and pulled out two nutrition bars. He handed one to his son and bit into the other. The boy took his and began to eat. The sounds of their chewing filled the emptiness of the temple. Adrian closed his eyes again and tried to recall the piano playing in the hall, but nothing came to him this time.

"Antoine?"

"Yeah, Dad."

"Do you listen to much music?"

"Music? Sure, all the time."

"What kind of music?"

"I don't know. Stuff." He shrugged and continued chewing.

"Do you ever listen to classical music? Concertos?"

"Oh, that stuff. Sure. Our teacher makes us listen sometimes."

"Do you like any of it?"

"It's all right, I guess."

Adrian chewed some more, swallowed, then took another bite from his bar.

"Dad?" Antoine said.

"Uh, hum."

"When do I get my wings?"

Adrian waited until he swallowed his mouthful before he answered.

"I hope never."

"But why?"

"These are weapons, Antoine. They are for fighting. I don't want you to fight."

"I can learn how to fight."

"I know you can, son. That's not the point." Adrian looked up, struggling to find the words. "Antoine, I want you to have a good life. A safe life. Taking up these wings will only lead to one thing, and I don't want that for you. I know your mother wouldn't want it either."

"How can you know *what* she wanted for me?"

Adrian sighed. Bested by a child. It was true he couldn't know what she wanted. He never had a chance to ask her. But he knew how he felt. The idea of his son flying out there and fighting god-knows-what chilled him to the bone. His son. *His* son. His dear, dear boy. The very image of his mother with almond-shaped eyes and skin so clear and brown. He loved him more than he thought was possible. His beautiful, beautiful boy.

"Antoine, I'm very tired. It's been a long day. We can talk more about this in the morning."

The overcast morning crept in holding hands with the night. The day began dark with hints of becoming darker. The mist swept over the river and brought with it the strong smell of burnt ash. The temple area was dreamlike and lush with pigeons fluttering above and little brown birds pecking at the crumbs he and Antoine had left behind. Adrian stared at his son lying on the stone floor and marveled at his beauty. His perfection. The sun broke through the clouds outside and shined a spot of light through the broken glass. For a moment his son was his mother. Adrian blinked and saw his son again.

Through the glass where a forest had been in the night was now a cleared field of emptiness. Adrian carefully stepped over sharp broken glass that crunched, split, and cracked under his feet to stand by the window's edge. The green forest outside was gone. All that was out there was a wasteland and fog. But what of the elk? He was sure that he had seen the elk. He looked again for a moment. The sound of Antoine stirring made him return to the stone temple.

"Hey, son. You sleep okay?"

Antoine nodded. Adrian pulled out his last nutrition bar and handed it to his him.

"Thanks, Dad."

Adrian stretched, then picked up his wings to check them. There were a few missing feathers from the edges and a dent on the side plating that he hadn't noticed before.

"Dad, aren't you gonna eat something?"

"Oh, I ate earlier," he lied as he bent the plating over his knee and began smoothing out the curve in the metal with the heel of his hand.

"Are we going home today?"

"I plan to," Adrian said. "Only we can't go back the way we came."

"Why?" Antoine asked.

"That area is probably being watched. We can't take a chance that things will follow us."

"Oh," Antoine said. "So how we getting home?"

"There are a few other entrances. And some of them only me and a few others know about. We're going home through one of them."

"Which one?"

Adrian thought on this for a few moments.

"I'm not sure yet," he said. "The safest one."

He lifted up his wings to shoulder height and looked them over. The brass-looking metal shined and glittered even in the dimness of the temple.

"I think I'll take you by way of the shipyards. You want to see the spaceships being built?"

"Sure!"

"There's an entrance over there with a lot of people protecting it. I think that's the best way."

Antoine wiped the corners of his mouth with his fingers.

"Dad?"

"Yeah."

"What do you suppose happened to everybody else? Did you think the roaches got 'em?"

"I don't know," Adrian said as he pounded on his wings some more. "I doubt it. They're good men. I'm sure they got away."

"Do you think the roaches are still outside?"

"The roaches don't like the light. We'll be okay now that it's the daytime. Come," Adrian said reaching out his hand, "help me put this on."

Antoine stood up and watched his father lift and position the wing harness on his back. Adrian allowed his son to fasten the lower buckles on his thighs.

"Dad."

"Yeah?"

"I wanna learn how to fly."

Adrian looked down on his son and saw the desire lying deep behind the request. He bent low so that he could face his son eye to eye.

"There are many ways to fly, Antoine. One way is with these wings on. Another is with your mind, and that's the greatest way. To see things that others can't and make them real with your hands, makes you soar higher than any bird—and greater than anything that can take a life, like me in this thing. That's what I want for you. I want to show you how to fly the right way. These wings aren't real, son. Only your mind is real."

Father and son walked hand in hand out to the main lobby that was still wet from the nighttime rain. In the light of day, without the tricks of shadow to hide the damage, the structure of the museum was more haunting. The old world was truly gone. Adrian helped his son wrap his crimson cloth around his face, and he wrapped his own around his. Then they went out the grand doors to face the mist. Outside they were greeted by a fractured, beaten boulevard once called the great Museum Mile. The mist smoked and swirled near the surface of the cracked paving stones, pooling around their feet.

Adrian picked up Antoine.

"I want you to hold on tight," he said. "Never let me go. Understand?"

Antoine nodded and grabbed his father around the neck. Adrian embraced his son and nuzzled him, feeling his child's heartbeat next to his. *I will get my child home safe.*

He opened his wings, stretching them wide to catch the wind. They *shinged* and tinkled, and he ran holding his son. The air lifted them, and they ascended high and higher. The rush of the breezes sped past his cheeks. He held onto Antoine and coasted, curving around to head north toward the shipyards. He could see the ribs of the ships poking up through the light mist of the morning. A dot of green appeared in the air. It was flat with no depth, yet it seemed as real as the clouds that floated past. Adrian steered to avoid it.

Before them was the wall that Adrian had designed to protect the ships. It was still under construction, yet it already seemed to stretch from one end of the island to the other. On the other side of it was civilization. It was an impenetrable barrier between the craziness that the world had become and calm order. Fortresses were placed every mile along its perimeter, each housing several fighting men to defend the border. Once they reached one of those fortresses, his son would be safe.

"Dad!"

Adrian looked to where Antoine was pointing. Creatures were closing in from behind. The aliens. The roaches. Maybe ten of them. They flicked and flittered through the air like a dark thought. Moving shadows that pierced through dimensional space.

Adrian tried to speed up. The shipyards were a little way ahead. He felt a tug at his leg. He shook it off and slashed it with released feathers that cut the thing in two. He held onto his son and screamed to the men working below. They were too far away and didn't seem to see or hear him. The creatures were around him, grabbing at Antoine, whose tight grip choked his neck.

Others in crimson and brass wings appeared. Maybe they had heard him after all. Maybe they had seen the struggle in the sky. Regardless, these were his people, and they had come to help him and his son. They flew up from below, mercilessly cutting. Adrian spun around and around, slicing as he went. How dare they attack him? How dare they attack his son? The boy slipped out of his arms. It was sudden. He just fell. Adrian tried to grab him, but couldn't find him. He looked all around. He couldn't see him. All was red and gold and screams and the sounds of slicing flesh, but his son was gone.

"Antoine! Antoine!"

17.

```
>>
>>
>> timeframe /jump +80

*SYSTEM TIMEJUMP COMPLETE*
.

.

.
```

Antoine was among eleven others in the elevator. A sadness lingered as they flew higher and higher, up to the surface. Flashes of light seeped through, periodically illuminating their somber faces as they passed the many levels of the underground city. Most of them looked like new recruits. Their young lineless faces stared aimlessly at the changing numbers indicating the levels as they went by. Antoine felt so old standing next to them. His stomach paunched over his belt, and his shoulders sagged. He had once had a body that was firm like theirs. But that was long ago. The years somehow had been stolen from him. It felt as though he had woken up one morning and found himself in this old skin. Being the son of "The Great Adrian," he had been permitted to come today as a courtesy. He knew his presence was not really needed, so he would do his best to stay out of the way. He wanted to see how all of this would play out. He wanted to see for himself how his world finally came to an end.

Antoine was old enough to remember when this was only a dream his father had. Now it was going to happen. And they were heading up to the surface for the last time to make sure all went well. The screeching inside the shaft sounded like a wailing child as the elevator reached the upper levels. Then the elevator was immersed in the natural light that shined in from above. Antoine leaned over to look out the windows in the door. They had reached the crust, the level between the very top of the city and the surface of the world. Stretching as far as his eyes could see were the great sheets of translucent metal used to produce the illusion of sky for the city below. They lay flat against the upper surface of the artificial world, undulating to simulate the movement of the heavens. Antoine could also see the inner workings of the atmospheric processors and the climate controllers that created the wind and the rain from the recycled air. No one was allowed to see this level. No one from the city was allowed out into the real world anymore. The high council had ordered it so. And who would disagree? No one really wanted to see the mess that had been made of it.

Antoine's dad had helped to design and build the underground city. He had been one of the few who understood that this day would be coming. If not for men like his dad, the fate of the people of Earth would be most uncertain. His dad had long ago passed on, killed when Antoine was a little boy of eight. Antoine knew his time was coming soon to join him. He wondered if his dad ever knew that he had taken him home safely that day. When Antoine saw him, he would tell him. There was so much that he wanted to tell him. He was almost looking forward to it. But mostly, he just wanted to see his dad again. He missed him so.

Antoine also wished that his dad could see the results of his work. The world as it once was had been recreated to the finest detail. Antoine had watched the city grow from a deep, wide chasm in the ground to what it was today. The tall buildings reaching into the artificial sky, the ordered and perpendicular streets, and the market square teeming with buyers and sellers, all gave the sense of once-was. The city dwellers could almost forget that they lived underground. The one criticism Antoine had was that the city seemed too clean. It lacked grittiness. It lacked "warmth." A city grown through the generations had a kind of disorder and randomness to it—a feeling that there might be something new and unexpected to be found by turning a corner and walking down an unknown street. The architecture of the underworld was too homogeneous, and so were the people. The young probably didn't regret living in a false environment. But Antoine always did. He still remembered the feeling of the real wind on his cheeks and the smell of the natural air.

Antoine changed his mind then. He was glad that his dad was not alive to see this day.

The elevator door opened on the surface level to a dark enclosed passageway. There was a hint of light from the other end of the hall. Everyone paused. No one said anything. Antoine waited for the first of them to leave the elevator. The youngest one walked out first, followed by the others. The air felt hot and dry and still as they walked toward the light. They stopped beside a small stairway that led to a door outlined by the glow of day. One of them produced a key card that glowed red on its edge. He slid the key into the slot next to the door, and a heavy lock clicked. Then the metal door slowly rumbled open, allowing in the hot fresh air. Sand and brown dirt flew toward them. One by one they climbed the stairs to emerge outside. Antoine struggled with every step he took. His knee joints creaked painfully. The young ones attempted to help him climb the stairs. Antoine refused their assistance. He wanted to do this himself.

Outside a watercolor wash of an orange-gray sky blotted out the sun. The twelve stood upon a landscape created by swirled dunes of sand. Earth had been completely transformed through the long years of Antoine's life. It was hard to believe that where he stood had once been a city. Today more than any other Antoine felt how his fate had been intertwined with that of his world. They had endured the last hard years together, and soon they both would pass away.

The air was arid and harsh against his skin. The twelve put on their veils. Antoine's veil dropped away from his face. He moved it back. He still found it foreign to drape a cloth across his nose and mouth. The young men didn't seem to have this problem. Their veils remained firmly in place, making them look like robbers with their faces almost completely covered with only a small space left for their eyes.

Antoine noticed that they were staring off into the distance behind him. He turned around to see where they were looking. There stood *The Trajan*, the last of the great ships. Its huge form darkened the landscape. It was as high as a building of once-was and as long as a farmer's field. The curve of its bow and the lift and sweep of its stern made it seem ready to take flight. It had all the hallmarks of his dad's designing hand.

Gathered beneath a wing of *The Trajan* was a large group of people sitting on the sand. The women wore dresses that had now become traditional, gonars, colorful robes that covered them from head to foot. The gonars were beautiful from a distance, in saturated colors such as purple, orange, and gold. The men dressed in gonars of solid white. All wore veils to protect their faces from the blowing sand and the dust. It was a treat for the eyes to see them. The people of the underground city had long ago decided on a more practical and drab form of dress.

Their arrival signaled the people to stand. Long gonars flapped in the heated breeze like waving flags. A few of the men remained to guard the door to the city while the others walked to the crowd, who waited in eerie silence the long moments it took for them to approach. The crowd parted noiselessly, allowing them to pass. There was only the sound of feet crunching in the sand. The men began to put up the temporary shelter, basically a large tent, to house the administrators once they arrived. Antoine stood aside and watched. It wearied him to see the young running around while he did nothing.

The people formed a line as if they were familiar with the routine. Here today were those who had waited until the very last possible moment to leave. They had probably thought that it would not come to this. But it had. The tickets that were once freely available to anyone who registered were gone. Many in line had not registered at all and were now vying for the few empty spots left. Antoine could pick out the ticketless on sight. They shifted and moved nervously while standing in line with shared expressions of terror. Many had small children with them. They waited peacefully for their chance to be put into the lifepods of *The Trajan* and hoped for the long cryogenic sleep that would take them to a new home. Antoine studied their veiled faces. So many. So many. The administrators would try to find a place for everyone. It was possible that there would be many left behind. This would take a long time to sort out, maybe all day. There was nothing to do but wait. Good luck to them. Good luck to them all.

When Antoine was a boy, he used to envy those leaving. His stomach welled with excitement just thinking about it. But as the years went on, he came to the conclusion that he didn't want to go, that he didn't want to be chased off his homeworld. He took the vow like many others to remain on Earth until the end of his days. It was like a religion. Do you believe in Earth, or don't you? Will you stay and defend her, or will you go? Earth first, Earth always—that's what the oath takers said, and Antoine agreed. The creatures had left Earth, but if they ever returned they vowed to defend her.

But the days of arguing were done. Today was the last day. Either you were on *The Trajan* or you were staying. It was that simple.

Antoine felt a pang of guilt. It had been his father's wish that his son go to the stars. The shades of doubt grew ever more dark in his mind. Maybe he should do as his father requested. He blinked the thought away.

One of the young men noticed Antoine standing alone. He walked over and gently touched Antoine on the arm. The boy had taken off his veil, revealing his heavy-lidded eyes. His head was round and shaped as if it were sculpted out of stone, his skin perfectly smooth. "Elder, maybe you should sit inside the shelter?" The boy attempted to guide Antoine into the tent.

"No, I'm fine where I am," Antoine said. "Thank you for your concern."

The boy took a stance that said that he wasn't going away. They remained standing together in an awkward silence. Antoine scratched at the skin under his beard. His veil dropped down again. He moved it back into place.

Antoine didn't really regret the vow he had taken all those years ago. He wondered sometimes if maybe he should have become a man more like his father, a man of quiet strength who bore the burdens of his life with a silent dignity. His dad was the greatest man Antoine had ever known. He hoped that he had told him that at least once. Maybe he could tell him that soon.

"Walk with me...uh? What is your name?"

"My name is Eliel."

"Eliel," Antoine paused for a moment, "I think that means 'consoler.'"

"Yes," Eliel smiled, "so my mother has told me."

Antoine took slow deliberate steps, and the boy followed close behind. They stopped and gazed at the long horizon. Antoine had roamed this very area when he was a young man. There were birds and green growing things then. He remembered the blue and the soft white clouds that floated through the sky like pulled cotton. That was in the days when he could still walk with a sense of unhurried freedom. But even then the sand had been encroaching from the west.

In the distance used to be a city. The hulking remains of it jutted out along the horizon at weird angles. He and his dad had visited once when great structures soared high into the air. All of that was gone now. His father had called it Elysium, land of the heroic dead. The sand and the dust had done their mighty work. Some of the buildings had been torn down for the metal they would provide. The others were left to rot and were worn away by the unending storms. All that would be left of this world soon would be the memories of old men like Antoine. And no one knew better than he that before long even that would be gone.

"Are you all right, Elder?"

"I am fine, Eliel. I was just thinking about something."

Antoine watched as more people from the underground arrived. They seemed to be coming from all sides at once, one by one and in pairs. They walked among the crowd, helping to carry their stores onto the ship, checking their tickets, or idly standing around. Antoine wondered if they had come for the same reason he had. Many seemed to have nothing much to do.

Antoine's veil slipped once more so that he had to maneuver it back into place. It felt silly to be constantly playing with the thing. When it dropped again, Antoine decided to leave it be and wear his face naked.

"Eliel," Antoine said, "do you ever question your decision to stay on Earth?"

"Elder?" Eliel said. He looked at the old man with a kind of shock. Antoine was sure that the boy was wondering about the soundness of his mind.

"Don't look so surprised. You *should* question it. You should question it every day. I have," Antoine said. "It will keep you centered. It will keep you whole." The last part felt crass and empty even as it passed his lips. That was the rhetoric he was supposed to say, but it was not how he actually felt. Questioning had kept Antoine far from centered. He had been feeling confused of late. This at a time in his life when he thought he should have a lot of the answers. The ideology that had sustained him all these long years was now losing its potency. Antoine wasn't sure about anything anymore. Maybe the boy would find better answers than he had.

"But Elder," Eliel said, "aren't you happy in your vows?"

"Happiness is..." Antoine said. "Happiness is an elusive thing."

He wanted to say something else. He thought he knew what, but the words got caught in his throat. Antoine walked on and Eliel followed him. They climbed to the top of a dune where they could see the queue of people boarding the ship. The long colorful line was beginning to disappear into *The Trajan*. It seemed to be swallowing them whole.

"Someone is coming," Antoine said.

Eliel shaded his eyes and looked all around.

"Where, Elder?"

"There." Antoine pointed to the faintest dot on the horizon. His ancient eyes were strong. "She will need our aid. Come."

Eliel obediently followed the old man down the dune, which gave way easily under each step. He offered Antoine his arm. Antoine was about to refuse Eliel's aid, but there was something in the boy's innocent expression that made Antoine release his pride. He had been self-sufficient all his life. He never thought of himself as someone who needed anyone's help. Maybe today was the day to put down old foolish ways.

The long blue gonar of the approaching woman fluttered in the wind like a sail. She held a small child on her hip. The closer she came into view, the easier it was to see the wariness in her slumping movements. Her child, a little girl, grasped at her mother's flowing robe and buried her head within her mother's veil. Antoine made his way to cross her path, with Eliel not far behind.

"Please," she said, "I know I am late. I tried, but my husband won't come. I…please… I don't have tickets. Please…"

Antoine gently said, "Come with me and Eliel here. We will take you to an administrator. Eliel, ease her burden and take the child." Eliel did as he was told, and the girl went to him without any fuss. The little thing wanted nothing more than to sleep and was forcing her eyes to stay open. Antoine patted the girl on the head as she rested in Eliel's arms, then he slowly guided his new charges to the tent.

The administrator stopped everything he was doing to listen to Antoine explain the woman's situation. Antoine had influence as the only son of one of the greatest of The Builders. Sometimes Antoine wondered if things would have been different if he had not been his father's son. Maybe his life would have been much harder. He was never quite sure. The administrator asked for the woman's name and wrote it down in his manifest. He said that he would try very hard to see that she and her child had a place in the ship. She took the news with gratitude, and Antoine led her to a seat inside the shelter.

The ship was due to leave in the evening, and it was getting dark. The faint radiance of the moon lay heavy on the horizon. There was a musty scent in the air. It was as if whatever moisture left in the sky released itself as the day cooled down. Antoine suddenly could breathe easier. A small wind picked up some sand in front of the tent and tossed it back and forth. It gave birth to a dancing brown dust faerie that swirled and twisted to the music of the moving air. Antoine followed the dust lady as she pirouetted, bowed, and curtsied to an invisible band. She swirled and turned and turned until she dissipated into nothing.

There were only a few people left standing in line. Because the wind had died down a bit, many pulled back their veils, revealing their wary faces. Their gaunt appearance spoke of the growing hunger rumored to be spreading among the aboveground population. The woman next to him sat in silence with her sleeping child. Together she and Antoine watched the endless flow of people as they entered one end of the shelter and exited the other to go up the gangway into the ship.

The mother pulled her veil back. Antoine could see her jawbones. Terror was written in the deep lines of her forehead and in the creases around her mouth. She seemed to be aging by the moment, though she did have a beauty to her. Her eyes were wide and dark, and her lips shimmered with neatly applied gloss. The intricate pattern woven into the delicate material of her gonar displayed high-quality workmanship. She must be a woman of some means. Antoine thought that she must find it strange to be in the position of begging for help. He was glad he could be there for her. It made him feel useful.

She got up to move nervously to the edge of the tent. She placed her hand on her mouth. It seemed as though she wanted to stop herself from saying something inappropriate. She was afraid. Those left behind on the surface would have to struggle to survive on the land. No one knew better than Antoine how they would fail.

"What is taking them so long?" she said.

"Patience. They will get to you in time," Antoine said.

The little girl was awake now, but she was quiet and spoke mostly with her eyes. She climbed onto Antoine's lap and leaned into the folds of his shirt to gently pull at his gray whiskers. Antoine put his hand before his face, then took it away quickly and softly said "shoo" to her giggles. As Antoine played this little game, her mother stared off into the administrator's direction. He wished he could know how it would all turn out. What would become of this little girl? Would she get to grow old like him? He held her tight, then pressed her nose like a button. She giggled and patted him on his tummy.

An administrator approached the woman. Her eyes were wide and haunted. She watched his every move like a timid animal. He whispered words to her. Antoine could not hear what was being said. He only saw him give her something. She took the man's hand and pressed it to her face. The administrator desperately tried to pull his hand away, but before he could she had already kissed his palm. Her gonar rustled as she bent over to gather her daughter out of Antoine's arms.

"Thank you," she said, her eyes glistening. With her warm lips she pressed hard against Antoine's forehead. A flush of heat warmed his cheeks. The little girl waved goodbye as her mother's back disappeared up the gangway and into the ship. Antoine raised his hand to return her farewell. He wondered if they would remember him. Probably not. Where they were going, they would have plenty of things to think about rather than the memory of an old man. Antoine tried to picture them on their new world. By the time they got there, he would have long since passed away. This ground would hold his bones.

Many still waited in line when the door to *The Trajan* closed. The people, once quiet and calm, pushed forward in a wild blur. A riot of color raged, turning and running and pushing. They tore at the tent, bringing it crashing down. Eliel grabbed Antoine by the arm to drag him behind a wall of men of the city, who had positioned themselves behind the crowd. A crazed woman lunged at Antoine. She came so close that he could smell her hot breath. Eliel struck her hard, and she fell to the ground. Blood flowed from a gash on her forehead. Antoine's heart felt as if it would burst out of his chest, it was pounding so hard. He was as helpless as a child. Eliel covered him. Protected him. Antoine was grateful and ashamed.

"You will all stop!" an administrator screamed. He stood on the gangway of *The Trajan*. The resonance of his voice carried into the night. "You will stop this!"

Everyone went still.

"You all knew that this was a possibility! You knew! We warned you! We urged you to prepare, but still you did nothing! Now there is no room! And there is nothing more that can be done! Return to your homes! We've done all that we can! Now return home and try to make the best of it! Just go home!"

The crowd remained motionless. A long tense time passed before anyone stirred. An army of men stood firmly between them and *The Trajan*. Antoine watched as the crowd slowly began to drift away and dissolve into the darkness until there was no one left. It didn't seem fair. None of this seemed fair at all.

The Trajan roared its engines and shook the ground. The vow keepers gathered together to stand before this last departing ship for their final prayer on the surface. Antoine covered his face with his veil and made his way slowly to the semicircle they had formed. They waited patiently for him to join them, their veils flapping in the breeze. *The Trajan* lifted up, sending a mighty storm of dust scattering in all directions. The sound of its departure troubled the ear like water to a drowning man.

They all looked up—except for Antoine. He looked only at his people. Many of them wept as they watched the ship ascend higher and higher into the night sky until it finally disappeared from sight. There were no tears for Antoine. He felt only hollowness. He thought he should want to cry. But he didn't.

Antoine waited with Eliel as the others disappeared into the many entrances to the underground. They were among the last to make their way down. Antoine's limbs ached with each step he made. Eliel and the others helped him inside. They handled him like a treasure. He didn't want their assistance, but he allowed them. It was time to let go. Antoine looked back once more at his world. It would be for the last time. A wind picked up and blew a gust of sand in his direction. Then he went inside and the door closed behind him.

```
>>
>>
>> timeframe /jump +200

*SYSTEM TIMEJUMP COMPLETE*

.

.

.


>>
>>
>> who

Tkeclc      observer    0000-00-00 00:00

>> change status Tkeclc interactive

*STATUS CHANGE SET*

>>
>> continue

BRIDGE PROCESS: CONTINUED
.

.

.
```

18.

Adrianne stared up at what others had either ignored or didn't notice, a tiny green dot. In her time of captivity she had seen it hovering in the air many times. It never moved. It never altered shape or size. It remained constantly in place, rain or shine. This anomaly was only one of many strange things about her surroundings. Three moons rose one after another to crisscross the night sky. The prison camp where they lived was gateless in a field of rock and dry red dirt. There was nothing around for miles and miles. It was a land of nothing. Or so it seemed.

Antoine lumbered over and put his large hand on her shoulder. She touched it and looked up into his round watery eyes. He had never been the same since he was wounded in the head in the fighting. It could have happened to anyone, but it had happened to him. Her big brother, who was always the one who knew what to do, now had a mind like a child.

"I'm hungry," he said.

"Then let's get something to eat."

They took their places in line to receive their meager food ration—a watery stew with chunks of God-knew-what in it. A bowl had enough nutrition to keep them from starving, but not much more than that. Antoine held his bowl with his head bent. Adrianne patted him on the tummy, reminding him that he would have food soon. He smiled a crooked smile, then laughed.

The krestge—the roaches—assigned one of her own people to pour out the stew—Tommy, a kid Adrianne knew from back home. She'd watched him grow up, and growing up wasn't so easy back home where every day was a fight to survive. The krestge's flickering shadowy bodies were everywhere on Earth now, squeezing all human life out of existence.

The morning after they arrived at the camp, they were marched, linked by chains, into the cold, miserable yard. The roaches pulled Tommy out of line, grunted in his face, and practically tossed him across the yard. Adrianne thought they were going to kill him. By instinct, she flipped over one of the guards and was headed for another before they knocked her down. When she came to, Antoine was bent over her, brushing her cheeks, shedding tears like a baby. Then she saw that they had handed Tommy a ladle and stood him before a hot caldron of stew.

Over and over again, she told Antoine that she was all right. She had to stand up straight to make him stop crying. Her whole body was a giant bruise, but she smiled so he smiled. It was funny to think that her stupid stunt was something that Antoine would have done if he had been in his right mind. That's what he always used to do, rush in without thinking. That was how he got hurt, and it was her who used to pick him up and worry.

Large rocks were scattered about the red ground. They used them as seats. The rocks were not quite comfortable to sit on but they were better than the ground. Adrianne found a rock and sat with Antoine not far behind, willing to sit on the dirt. They huddled together as best they could during meal times and talked in hushed tones, trying not to attract the attention of their captors. The stew smelled especially bad today. It slimed and plopped in her metal bowl, the chunks moving as if they weren't quite dead. Adrianne closed her eyes and ate. There were no utensils, so she ate with her hands, which were dirty since water was in short supply. At least the stew warmed her fingers.

"Hey, Antoine," Jolly whispered.

"Hey, Jolly!"

"Shh! Not so loud," Adrianne said.

Antoine put his index finger against his lips, which was formed into a little "o," then whispered, "Hey, Jolly."

Jolly patted Antoine on the back and leaned over to whisper in Adrianne's ear.

"Some of the guys slipped out last night."

"What?" she whispered back. "Damn. I told everyone to sit tight."

"No one seems to notice yet."

"Keep me posted, Jolly."

"Will do," Jolly said.

They all ate with their fingers. The stew was so watery it was more of a drink anyway. Antoine was playing with a chunk from the stew, and it wiggled on his fingers. Adrianne told him to stop messing with it and to just eat. Her stomach soured when he popped the thing in his mouth.

Jolly tapped Adrianne to get her attention. "Look what's comin' for dinner?"

She looked to where his head was pointed and saw what everyone else saw, a new prisoner being escorted through the gate.

"What the hell?" Adrianne said under her breath.

The roaches were escorting one of their own into the compound, pulling it along in chains. The Krestge were four-dimensional creatures. To human eyes, parts of them seemed to disappear into shadow as they moved. But this new one was different. It was more solid than the others, its planar shifts more defined and less shadowy. It emitted pale, weak colors and looked sick or beaten or both. They threw it to the ground, nearly missing a bunch of rocks that could have split its head open.

"Nice," Jolly winced.

"Yeah," Adrianne said.

The krestge prisoner struggled to stand up. Nobody moved to help. They watched as it stumbled to its feet. It seemed dazed. When it was fully erect, it stared over at her people. Adrianne could almost make out the thing's expression. Some of the humans turned their backs; the krestge guards walked away. It looked around, then climbed onto a group of rocks and sat down.

"Whaddaya suppose that's all about?" Jolly asked Adrianne.

"I have no idea."

A freezing wind blew, causing knuckles to crack and faces to peel. They made gloves out of the thin cloth of their blankets.

Wearing them didn't give them much warmth. The cloth seemed to protect their skin a little, though. They cut the tips off the gloves so that their fingers could handle things easier and took them off when it was time to eat. It had become habit to put her numb fingertips in her mouth to breathe heavily on them. Her hands were filthy. It didn't matter. They were the only fingers she had.

Antoine rocked himself and played with his nose. Adrianne moved his hand away from his face and wiped his fingers with her shirt. A deep scar snaked across his forehead. The result of the accident that had crippled his mind. She caressed his scar, then took him into her arms and held him close. He needed her to baby him like a child. And this she would do until her dying day. Dear sweet, sweet Antoine.

"So what's the news?" Adrianne whispered to Jolly.

"No news is good news. The guys are still AWOL."

"No sign of them, huh? At least that's something."

She wished they'd listened to her and waited. Adrianne wanted to make a real break from this hellhole, taking the rest of her people with her. But she needed time to figure out where to go. There were those who'd escaped and were never found. She couldn't figure out where they had gone. The escaped guys must have figured out something, she thought. Adrianne did her morning check. Around them there was only a flat horizon and a desolate heavy sky. And there it was—the green dot. Same place. Same size. Same everything.

"Look at that thing over there," Jolly said.

For a moment Adrianne thought Jolly was talking about the green dot, but his eyes were focused on the other side of the camp where the krestge prisoner sat on a rock. It was bent over, bluish where it should be purple, and shaking like it had a fever.

"Why doesn't it get something from the pot?" Steven said.

"It looks sick," Tommy said.

"Serves it right," Jolly said.

"Maybe it's too sick to get up?" Tommy said.

"Maybe we should get him something to eat or something," Steven said.

"Whaddaya nuts?" Jolly said. "I wouldn't lift my dick to piss on it."

Jolly was a great fighter. He followed orders without questions, and if Adrianne told him to, he'd run straight into hell. But sometimes he made her feel crazy with his stupid talk. She stood up, went to the pot, scooped some of the so-called stew into a metal bowl, and walked over to the krestge. Antoine lumbered behind her, looking away from the creature and rubbing his nose.

"Ya want something to eat?" Adrianne said and waved the bowl in front of the krestge to get its attention.

It looked up. There was something in the way it stared at her that made Adrianne think of her cat back home. It was as if the creature understood you better that you realized and was surprised and grateful at the unexpected kindness from a lower being.

It took the bowl and nodded. It scooped some of the stew with its fingers and chewed slowly. It didn't seem to like the stuff either, but it ate. Adrianne watched it for a bit, then she and Antoine returned to their own kind. She looked back and saw that the krestge was still eating while it stared off into space.

The three moons sat heavy and low in the dim morning sky. They had aligned themselves into an isosceles triangle. Each was a different color—orange, yellow, and the one highest in the sky, a deep purple. The krestge forced everyone out of their beds into the open area of the camp. The humans and the one krestge prisoner were lined up to face the moons and made to bow while the guards hummed what Adrianne figured were their prayers. Adrianne ventured to look around. Her eyes locked onto the krestge prisoner. The thing seemed to be smiling at her.

With the humming over, the guards replenished the pot of stew. Maybe it was some kind of religious sacrament for the krestge to feed them. Whatever the reason, Adrianne was glad for the additional food. The last few days the men had been scraping at the bottom, eking out what they could. It was slop, but it did fill the belly. The men lined up to get their share of the muck from the cauldron. The krestge prisoner joined them.

"I don't like this thing near me," Jolly said under his breath.

"Take it easy, Jolly," Adrianne said and maneuvered herself to stand next to the krestge. "It's just as much a guest here as you and I."

"Shit," Jolly said, "how can you stand the smell?"

"Jolly, shut it."

Jolly frowned, but did what he was told. Antoine laughed and rubbed his nose. Adrianne tapped his stomach to make him stop.

"Feeling better I see," Adrianne said to the krestge. It made a small grunt and held out its bowl. Adrianne couldn't tell if it was a friendly wave or a brush off. It received its portion of stew and retreated slowly to its rock on the other side of the yard.

"Whaddaya suppose is the deal with him?" Steven said. "I mean, what's he doing here?"

"Good question," Adrianne said. A portion of the slop was poured into her bowl, and she tugged at Antoine's arm to tell him to follow. They walked toward the alien and sat on the ground before it. The krestge stared at them and gently nodded as Adrianne scooped some of the food into her mouth with her fingers.

"Hu-man~~," the krestge said.

Adrianne looked up.

"You speak, and English at that."

"I speak~~ma-ny lan-gua-ges~~," It said. "How~~ma-ny you~~ speak?"

Antoine laughed.

"You got me there. I usually have a translator in my ear," Adrianne said, looking around, "but around here, no such luxuries."

"Yes~~~lux-ur-ies here~~are rare.~~"

She studied it, looking for where the sound was coming from. All she could see were moving shadows flowing around it. Her eyes could not fix on its shifts through four dimensions.

"So what the hell are you doing in this piss-hole?"

The krestge moved its shoulders up and down as if it had the shivers. It took a moment for Adrianne to realize that it was laughing. She smiled, and Antoine laughed.

"Hu-man~~, you have a way~~with your lan-guage!" it said. "And you~~~are quite~~ how do you say?~~a-stute.~~"

It shook for a few more moments then answered, "I make~~mis-take.~~You make mis-take. You pay~~for mis-take. So~~I am here.~~"

"What kind of mistake, if I may ask?" Adrianne said.

"I am~~an aca-demic—a research-er. I ask~~~uncomfor-table ques-tions~~on treat-ment of hu-mans."

"You consider that a mistake?"

"Perhaps~~I should ask~~~ques-tions with~~more delicacy.~~"

Adrianne considered the krestge before her for a moment. The more she stared at it, the more its planar shifts moved. She could see the thing for what it was behind the shadows of shifting form. It was a creature trying to survive, just as she and her people were.

The krestge stopped eating and said, "Per-haps, I should~~be ask-ing that~~~of you." He pointed its long finger. "Why~~are you~~~here?~~"

"Why do you think?" Adrianne said and shoved more food into her mouth. Some of the stew escaped onto her chin. She used her arm to wipe it away.

"This is not~~an an-swer to~~~the ques-tion.~~"

"We're flyers," Adrianne used her hand to show the swooping and sailing of flight, opening her fingers wide like feathers. "And I killed a lot of your people."

"Of this~~you are~proud?~~~"

Adrianne put down her bowl.

"Yeah, quite proud. If you hadn't attacked us in the first place…"

The krestge held up his four-fingered hand. "You say~~attack. Our history~~~says at-tempt at~~con-tact. We~~de-fend our-selves.~~"

"That's bull! You're a bunch of butchers and liars. You find a nice blue planet. Only one problem, there are already people living on it. So you decide to dust us out like vermin. That's what you call us, right? Vermin."

"I am~~aware of a parti-cular~~~name for us~~you call."

"Roaches. And that's what you are, roaches crawling into places where you don't belong."

Adrianne stood up. Antoine began to cry. She tapped to make him stop.

"Did you expect us to just let you move in? To leave our home without a fight? Yeah, I fought you. And I'll continue to fight you with everything I got."

Antoine's face was scrunched up like he had eaten a lemon. He held back his tears. Adrianne took his hand and walked back to the others. She turned around to see that the krestge was quietly continuing its meal as if it was already thinking about other things.

At night, the air was still. Nothing moved. The only sound was the heavy breathing of the sleeping krestge. Adrianne turned over on her bunk to where it was cool and touched her harsh pillow. She thought of Helen and the smell of her hair and the lotion she put on her face at night that smelled of too-sweet flowers. Sometimes Adrianne liked to touch her when she slept just to feel her warmth and the rhythm of her pulse. Adrianne wanted to get back to her. If only Adrianne knew that she was all right—that Earth was all right—she could bear this place.

"Adrianne, you awake?" Antoine whispered.

"Yeah, I'm awake," Adrianne whispered back. "How can anyone sleep over that racket?"

The snores of the krestge rose and fell like a rolling sea.

"I've been thinking about home," Antoine said.

"Yeah, me too."

"You suppose they're okay?"

"I dunno." Her voice trailed away.

Helen had never liked Antoine, and now that he was injured Adrianne supposed that she would like him even less. It was something irreconcilable between them. It was why Adrianne left with Antoine to go fight, leaving Helen behind. Truth be told, even without the war there was probably not a home to go back to. It didn't matter, though. Adrianne still dreamed of Helen.

"Try to get some sleep, 'Twone," she said.

Steven stumbled to Adrianne's bunk and shook her urgently whispering, "They caught the guys."

"What? Are you sure?"

"They're bringing them in now."

Adrianne and eight others rushed to the window. The four who had escaped were being marched into the yard. One of the four was Kim. Adrianne considered him a good friend, and he was only a kid. For a moment their gazes met. Adrianne imperceptibly lifted her chin so that watching eyes wouldn't notice. Kim understood the gesture's meaning and nodded in return. They were led to one of the empty barracks to await judgment.

"What are they going to do to them?" Antoine whispered, his voice shaking.

"I don't know," Adrianne said.

"I think they kill prisoners who try to escape," Steven said.

"They won't," said a-prisoner-who-didn't-talk-too-much. "They can't... Can they?"

"I don't know if they would do that, Steve," Adrianne said.

"It's still possible," Steven said. "We don't know their rules of war."

The simple truth was finally stated. Their position finally uttered. They had no freedom. Their lives were completely at the mercy of these people who weren't people. Their prison, their rules. Any sense that they had any control over their situation was an illusion. They belonged to the krestge, and their lives were subject to their whims. Someone had tried to escape. Someone had to pay. Someone had to be sacrificed.

Antoine cried.

Two days later, in the middle of the night, Adrianne and the others were led into the yard. Nine prisoners stood at attention to watch. Two were more than friends. One had curly-red-hair-that-was-slowly-turning-auburn. One was Steven the brave. One was the krestge. One had gray-eyes-who-didn't-speak-too-much. One was a direct descendant of Dionne Maiter. The last were Adrianne and Antoine. They were a vigil in rags. The drizzle steadily soaked through what was left of their clothing, the rain commingling with the wetness already on their faces.

In the darkness lit only with powered torches, the prisoners were made to form a semicircle around four posts set in the middle of the yard. The wood looked new, as if cut recently.

No one spoke. Adrianne couldn't swallow as they watched the guys who had escaped hauled into the muddy open yard, handcuffed, wearing nothing but filthy underwear, exposing all their shame. They shivered from the cold and the fear. Antoine clasped Adrianne's hand. It was a high offense to try to escape. There was only one other thing a prisoner could do that was worse, and that was to kill a krestge guard.

Adrianne did her best not to seem scared for the sake of Antoine. Though if it were possible to run, she would. In her mind she was already running and running and running so fast no one could catch her. She was running and soaring up into the air far toward the horizon. She was the wind. She could take flight.

Human prisoners were ordered to lug the escapees out to the posts. Tommy was one of those who was forced to pull and pull at the struggling prisoners. He looked up at Adrianne with fear in his eyes as he helped tie the struggling prisoners to the posts. The sounds of them whimpering tore at Adrianne's insides. *I'll fly away, O Lord. I'll fly away...*

"No, please, don't..." someone on the pole shouted. There was no one to help. Everyone knew it. He knew it.

The forced human guards had to cover their mouths. This only made the four shout more, even as their mouths were gagged.

One great morning when the world is over, I'll fly away... away, away, so far away I'd fly, and no one would ever catch me.

The krestge prisoner walked into the yard. It addressed the guards in their language. Adrianne couldn't understand but it seemed that it was pleading with them on the humans' behalf. The guards listened to it for a while then pushed it down and kicked it a few times. It limped away looking very hurt. Antoine began to cry. Adrianne tapped him in the stomach to tell him to stop.

The air was charged with static that pricked the skin. Adrianne had no idea what was going to happen next. Each guard stooped into the corner to pick up something. They reentered the circle and stood about six feet away from the posts. Adrianne squinted her eyes tight to make out the objects in their hands. They were leather whips. The whites of Kim's eyes glistened as a guard ripped off his rags, then the clothes of the guy next to him, then the next, and the next.

Adrianne began to sing—*My homeworld, 'tis of thee...*

The rest of the prisoners joined in singing in shaking voices—*Sweet land of Liberty...*

The first lash sent red rippling. The splatter of it stained the ground. A scream, even through the cloth tied around their mouths, pierced the ears. Adrianne sang louder to cover the echo—*Of thee I sing...*

The second lash—*Land where my fathers died*

The third—*Land of the Terrans' pride*

The fourth—*From every mountain side*

Lash after lash after lash after lash—*Let freedom ring...*

19.

Adrianne tore off a piece of a blanket to make a square of about a foot and a half on each side. She melted the boot heel from the discarded shoes of a dead prisoner and carefully traced out a nine-by-nine square checkerboard on her piece of cloth. Antoine watched quietly and wondered what she was doing. She spent all afternoon on her project, receiving only glances from her fellow prisoners and the guards.

After she was done, Adrianne went out into the yard and looked for rocks. There were plenty of small ones lying around. She showed Antoine the size rocks she was looking for—no bigger than her thumb tip. Together they searched for them, gathered them up, then sorted them: eighteen cream-colored rocks in one pile and twelve blackish ones in the other.

In the overcast sky, a few stars shined through. It took some time to find, but Adrianne's eyes spied the green dot. It was so small it was barely visible. Satisfied, she went inside the barracks with Antoine lumbering behind. She found the krestge lying on its bunk staring up at the ceiling and stood over it until it turned toward her. Its planar shift moved as it slowly sat up. It was eerie to look upon a creature that existed in multiple dimensions, shifting and changing, half in shadow even in full light.

"You ever play checkers?" she said.

"What is~~check-ers?"

"It's a game. I'll show you."

Adrianne laid her makeshift checkerboard on the bunk and sat down. Antoine sat down cross-legged on the floor, and together they poured their rocks on the bed and neatly placed the checker pieces in their beginning squares. Antoine seemed so pleased to be helping and laughed when he was done. The krestge looked on as Adrianne explained the game and made her first move.

"In-ter-est~~ing," the krestge said after a time, then moved a piece on the board.

Adrianne leaned over and moved another stone, jumping over the krestge's piece.

"You have games like this where you come from?"

"We have~~games such~~~~as this, yes—for child-ren.~~"

"Yeah, this is usually for kids on my world, too. But in this shit-hole we might as well do something."

They continued to move their pieces across the board.

"~~King me~~," the krestge said after making its latest move.

"Damn, you learn fast."

"Learn fast~~, yes."

Adrianne put one of her captured rocks beside the krestge's newly elevated rock. Antoine laughed.

"They really laid into you last night, didn't they?"

"Laid~~in-to~~me?"

"They kicked you bad. Howya feeling?"

"No~~need to~~wor-ry a-bout my~feel-ing. I~~will be~~~ well."

"I want to thank you for trying to stick up for my men."

"No need~~to thank. It~~~~was my duty.~~A-buse~~~of hu-mans was~~in-cor-rect. I was~~ un-a-ware of such~~~harsh treat-ment. Now, I see~~for my-self. For this,~~~I apo-lo-gize for my~~people.~~~"

They finished their game then began a new one, carefully setting up the pieces together.

"Who~~is this hu-man~~~who always~~fol-lows you?"

"He's my brother."

"What is~~wrong with him?~~~"

"Nothing's wrong with him!" Adrianne said sharply. Then she added, "He got hit in the head fighting your people."

"I see.~~~For this, I am~~also sor-ry."

Antoine laughed.

Heavy thick drops of icy rain fell the next day. The men shivered with bent necks and bowed heads as they waited in line for their share of stew. No one covered the pot, so water fell into it. Jolly said that he thought it made the stew taste better, like seasoning from above. Adrianne squinted at the darkened sky, unable to find the green dot. Then, as a cloud drifted past, a patch of light came through, and the small dot of green reappeared.

"Hey, man, you okay?" Tommy said.

"Yeah, I'm good."

"How's Kim doing?" Adrianne asked.

"I don't know, man." He nodded in a way that said that he *did* know. Adrianne gave him her metal bowl and walked toward the bunkhouse for the sick. Antoine tried to follow.

"Stay with Tommy," she said. He sniffled but stayed where he was told.

Kim and the others who'd been whipped lay on their stomachs. Their backs, exposed to the air, were ripped crimson and orange flesh as if a great force had violently ripped their wings off. Kim labored hard to breathe through his mouth. He could barely open his eyes.

"Hey, kid, howya doing?" Adrianne said.

"Hiya, not too good, ma'am..." Kim mumbled.

"Don't say that. You'll be right as rain in no time."

Kim grunted or something. Maybe it was an attempt at a laugh.

"Anything I can do for you?"

"No, Ma'am. Dank you..."

Adrianne bent down and put her face close to his.

"Kim, I want you to listen to me real careful, okay son? This is *very* important. I want you to tell me what you saw when you were outside the camp. And I mean everything. No detail is too small."

Kim swallowed and closed his eyes. He wet his lips and whispered, "At first, it was all rocks and stones, den I saw green, ma'am, just green."

The effort to speak took a lot out of Kim, Adrianne could see. She wanted to ask him more but decided that she would wait and talk to him later after he had rested. But Kim died in the night, and the guards took the body away. To where, no one asked. It didn't seem like it mattered. Dead was dead. His friends slowly burned his things to stay warm. Everything that they tossed onto the flames was like watching him die once more.

～

Adrianne considered the new dynamics of the game. The krestge was winning. It had won all of the last few games. She moved her man at the edge of the board over one spot, then saw a clear opening the krestge had made for her to jump two times and get kinged. She bit her lip and said nothing, hoping the thing would not see its vulnerable position.

"You are~~not what~~~I expect-ed," the krestge said.

"In what way?" Adrianne asked.

"You~~are so much like~~~naïve child-ren."

It made a move leaving its opening on the board. She wasn't sure if the thing did it because it felt sorry for her or because it truly didn't see. It didn't matter, Adrianne was going to use its lapse of judgment. She picked up one of her rocks and jumped over two of the krestge's pieces, then saw another opportunity to jump before she removed her hand.

"Hmm~~~," the krestge said. "I was~~not a-ware that this~~ you could do.~~"

"Now you know," Adrianne said. She collected three of the cream-colored rocks and put them with her recently diminished pile.

"You do know that we aren't actually here?" Adrianne said.

The krestge looked at Adrianne.

"What~~is it do you mean~~~by this?" the krestge said.

"I mean this place is not where we actually are."

The krestge put his four fingers on Adrianne's hand. "Yes~~, this I know.~~~How is~it that this~~you know as~well?"

Adrianne shrugged as if the confirmation of her theories didn't make her guts feel like melting and said, "I figure, we're in a projected environment of some kind."

"Hmm~~, may-be~~hu-man is not~~~so naïve af-ter~~all."

"So how'd you figure out this place ain't real?" Adrianne asked.

"This~~~is a perfect repro-duction~~of the nor-thern contin-ent~~of my home-world. In this~~~period of time, my~~people have des-troyed~~most of this~~~land."

"Destroyed? Whaddaya mean, destroyed?"

"This place~~was home~~ to dis-si-dent groups. We~~~ annihil-lated them~~and made this~~~land unin-habit-able," the krestge said. "There-fore~~, our sur-roundings~~~can-not exist."

"How did you do a thing like that?"

"Of all~~peoples, hu-mans~~~must know."

"Yeah," Adrianne said a little above a whisper. Her mouth went dry, and she thought of Earth. The krestge stared at Adrianne as if it could sense her discomfort.

"Do not~~look so con-cerned, hu-man. It is no~~more than they de-served. The~~~dis-si-dents commit-ted~~much worse atroci-ties~~~in their time."

Adrianne leaned back and rubbed her face, then looked away for a minute and said, "Why do you suppose they are doing all of this?"

It thought for a moment. "At this time~~in our history~~~, my people are reexamin-ing~~our relation-ship with~~the hu-mans~~~. Man-y dis-agree.~~Previous to~~this, soldiers such as yourself~~would not have been~~~kept alive."

Adrianne wiped her hands on her numb legs, stood to walk around to get the feeling back into them, and said, "So if we are not here, where are we?"

Adrianne walked out to the edge of the encampment. The moons shined high in the distance, and she was surrounded by shades and the irregular shapes of the rocks and the barracks. There was a chill. A wind had shifted over the horizon, causing a distortion in the landscape. An apparition of dust formed a glim-mer of green in the distance. She thought she saw something move—floating high above, dipping and swooping.

She went into the barracks and watched her brother sleep for a while. Antoine was such a beautiful man. It was hard to be-lieve that his mind had been so damaged. She missed his wit and charm, his quick comebacks and jokes. She missed talking to him about her fears and hopes, and the way he gave her comfort with his strength. Those late-night conversations when they dreamed of their world free of the krestge, humankind once again building cities filled with people and art and music. She took a few moments to compose herself and thought, better to risk it all than rot here.

She shook Antoine awake. His eyes opened wide in fear.

"Shh," she whispered, covering his mouth. "We're getting out of here tonight. Help me with the others."

"Hey," a voice behind her said. Adrianne couldn't see the source, but she knew it must be Jolly. She could feel his male bulk. "What's going on?"

"Get your things together. We're leaving." True to his nature, Jolly didn't question. He simply helped gather the others.

"Where's Steven?" Adrianne asked.

"He's left already."

"What?"

"He said he had to do something," the one-who-didn't-talk-too-much said.

"I~~wish also~~to come with~~~you," the alien prisoner whispered in his bunk.

"No way!" Jolly nearly screamed.

"Shh!" Adrianne said, and thought, if they left it behind, it could raise the alarm, and they would be caught before they even left. And it could be useful if they managed to get out of the camp with its intimate knowledge of the krestge.

"It comes with us," she said. She held up her finger to Jolly. "There is no negotiating this. We have a long night in front of us. Let's go."

They crossed the boundaries of the yard without notice. The group traveled in the silence and the dark for what felt like hours with no one behind them. It was strange that it was so easy to escape. She was ready for a fight that seemed like it was not going to come. The moons' failing light left them unable to see. The alien prisoner trailed behind. They waited as it shuffled over the dirt. When it approached them they said nothing and continued on together long into the night.

Before them appeared a large wall. It was old and seemed abandoned and was crumbling in several areas. It stretched from horizon to horizon with turrets every mile or so. It looked like her ancestor's wall. But it couldn't be, Adrianne thought. That wall was back home on Earth. She looked up into the empty sky and saw no stars, no moons, only deep, deep indigo as far as the eye could see.

A trench ran parallel the long distance before the wall. It would make the climb to the top even harder. Adrianne sighed and began to trudge forward when the ground began to rumble. A vibration that could be felt deep in the heart. Adrianne turned to see the guards coming for them. Shifting, flittering, more shadow than form, riding on the wind.

"Come on!" Adrianne called as she scrambled frantically over some rocks. Everyone ran. Jolly was way in front and arrived at the wall first. He stopped to help the ones behind him over the loose stones, screaming "Hurry up!" as if it were necessary. From where Adrianne stood, all there was to see was a haze of green. She could hear voices coming from the other side of the green. Antoine stood beside her, frozen, waiting for her to tell him what to do. Adrianne pushed Antoine over the wall and into the green. She looked around at the oncoming brood then jumped.
>>
>> .

1011000110110001101100011011000011 01
>>

She fell wrong on her foot, onto wet soil. Above her, running feet scuffled on the wooden planks. Her ankle hurt like hell, but she had to keep on moving. She was surrounded by slimy, smelly, nasty things. There was no time to think or feel or be scared. Only time to run and hide. She silently moved among the leaves. Lights were peering down from above. She was sullied with mud and muck as she went deeper and deeper into the reeds and mess. Someone jumped down, then someone else. She kept moving.

Then a flashlight was on her. They grabbed her. She fought like a cat. All went dark.

...one one zero zero zero one one zero one one zero zero zero one one zero one one zero zero zero one...

...light and colors with unfocused edges. Adrianne blinked several times and still she could not see clearly. She had a terrible headache, one that she felt on her ears and on the bridge of her nose. The fuzziness focused.

```
>>
>>
** BREAK **
```

```
1011000110110001101100011011000110
1000110110001101100011011000110110
0110110001101100011011000110110001
0110001101100011011000110110001101
0001101100011011000110110001101100
1101100011011000110110001101100011
1100011011000110110001101100011011
0011011000110110001101100011011000
1011000110110001101100011011000110
1000110110001101100011011000110110
0110110001101100011011000110110001
```

.
.
.

Twelve people surrounded her. Four were best friends. Two were more than that. One had curly-red-hair-that-was-slowly-turning-auburn. One was the Alien. One had gray-eyes-and-didn't-speak-too-much. One was a direct descendant of Dionne Maiter. The last was Antoine.

"She's coming to..." one said.

"Hey, there, we thought you were a goner..." said another softly.

"We made it, Adrianne," Antoine said then laughed.

"We made it because of you," Jolly said.

"Evidently~~~, you were correct about~~~the pro-jected en-viro-ment," the alien said. "No-thing~~in the camp~~~was real."

"I always knew you'd survive," Helen said. Adrianne touched Helen's face to feel the breath from her nose and mouth. She drank in her warmth.

"But..." Adrianne said, "something is wrong..."

"Nothing is wrong," Helen said. "Not with us. Everything is as it should be."

"Everything..." Adrianne touched the nape of Helen's neck, caressed her ear, then whispered tender words too deep to recall. She kissed Helen on the tip of her chin. Smoothed her eyebrows. Touched the back of her head and the softness of her hair. "Everything..."

Behind them Adrianne could see all the stars in a familiar nighttime sky with a single waxing moon. She had no words. This was Earth. She was home. She had always been home. Then, high in the distance, she noticed the smallest dot of green.

20.

The wind tasted of salt and the sea as moist air sailed through the window. The warmth of soft sheets and a thick blanket surrounded her. She stretched, feeling the crinkle and gentle pop of her muscles unstiffening. Then the smell of hair perfumed by lilac-scented shampoo. Adrianne reached over and held the warm body next to hers and sighed deeply. This was an amazing fantasy.

She felt Helen get out of bed, leaving the place where she once lay empty and warm. She watched her go into the bathroom and heard the sounds of the water pouring down. The cat made his appearance, jumping onto the bed, mewing and demanding his breakfast.

"Come on, little guy," Adrianne said as she slipped out of bed.

She and the cat went into the kitchen where she opened a can of food and emptied it into its flat ceramic bowl with the picture of a rotund kitty in the center. The cat ate hungrily, and it smacked and purred with delight.

A warm light came through the open kitchen window as a breeze flowed in. She could see the wall in the distance. Broken in areas, but still sound and strong against the cruel forces on the other side. Helen entered the kitchen in full military dress of crimson and copper shielding. She was buckling a belt around her waist.

Adrianne handed her a cup of coffee and poured one for herself. It had been so long since she tasted something this wonderful. It filled her with peaceful pleasure.

"We don't have much time before I have to be back on duty," Helen said. "The war is not going well."

"The war..." Adrianne said. So far away. Meaningless to her only hours before. Now it was everything.

"Then let's make the most of the time we have," Adrianne replied. She took Helen by the hand, and they sat down. Adrianne kissed her deeply. She tasted the sweet saltiness. The slip and moistness of her tongue in her mouth. Then she thought—she remembered—that this was wrong. None of this should be happening.

Helen pulled out of her arms. "I think you need to stay home and rest today."

"Don't worry," Adrianne said. "I'll take it easy."

"Good. I'll see you later on tonight, okay?"

This was not the Helen she knew. Her Helen would never don a uniform or patrol the wall. Adrianne smiled and held onto Helen's face for a moment longer, then let her go.

"When did you join the war effort?"

"Since after you went away," Helen said.

"I thought you hated the fighting."

"Really? You thought that about me?" She touched Adrianne on the chin. "I've always understood that it was necessary."

"I see."

She watched as Helen picked up the harness for her wings. They *shinged* as she lifted them.

"Helen."

"Yes?"

"You know that I've always loved you."

Helen smiled. "You don't even have to say it." Then she turned and marched out the door.

Alone in the kitchen, Adrianne spoke aloud, "I only wanted to tell you one last time."

Her favorite clothes lined the closet. Items that she remembered being long worn out or stained hung perfectly intact, ready for her to wear. She picked out an outfit and laid it on the bed and stared at it. Then she pulled out of her dresser some sweatpants, a T-shirt, and a warm pullover, put them on and was out the door.

Antoine was waiting for her on the front porch. He smiled when he saw her and hugged her like a bear.

"Where we going today, Adrianne?"

"We're going home, 'Twone."

He laughed.

"You so silly, Adrianne. We are home."

"No, baby, we're not."

She took him by the hand, and they walked together through the peaceful city. It was the city she remembered growing up in with her brother. Friendly faces smiled at them as they walked. Many of them seemed sickly and tired, yet they smiled and went about their daily business. Antoine was happy and swung his arms like a child. This was the place that serviced the men who patrolled the wall. Providing them with food and all the comforts of home. It was home, and Adrianne loved it. But it wasn't real.

Voices, accents, languages whose rhythms echoed places Adrianne had never seen (and never would) beat past her like a marching band. The sounds were a blending stream of conversations and sighs. The faces that passed her were from all over. Each a different shape and color. The smell of roasting peanuts on open charcoal burners, curried meats, and frying falafels drifted through the warm air. Adrianne and Antoine moved asynchronously in the uneven flow of people.

The open doors of the boutiques and electronic stores blasted icy wind from air conditioners set on super high. The cold drifted out, beckoning them inside. Adrianne relished the cool against her skin. Through their reflection on the window into a clothing store she could see the plastic people looking at the mannequins in their styled outfits. She told Antoine to wait outside while she went in.

In a few minutes, her body adjusted to the cold. She roamed through the racks of shirts, skirts, dresses, and pants as Antoine stood outside patiently waiting. The perfume of a passing salesgirl was a mixture of sea breezes and powder. She clicked her price gun on a tag.

A red and white blouse caught Adrianne's eye. She pulled it off the rack and held it up to the light. It was a flowing delicate faux silk blouse, long at the bottom, with buttons at the top. She put it next to her body in front of a mirror. It was too young for her. So she put it back on the rack without much care. She really shouldn't be here, she thought. Back out to the streets to a smiling Antoine.

There was a man selling newspapers on the corner. The headlines told of war in foreign lands.

Adrianne looked at the sky, and it was blue, blue, no sun just blue. And there was the spot of green. Never moving, never changing shape or size. She followed it like the slaves of old the northern star. Down the boulevard, they saw corner after street corner after street corner, on and on ad infinitum. It was all such a beautiful illusion.

Past the stores and past the tall glass and steel skyscrapers, then to the area of small red brick townhouses in the lower edge of the city near the river. This was a part of the city that she should never be in, but here they were. She'd never realized how empty the city was outside their neighborhood. Wind carried newspaper pages flapping through the desolate streets, the breeze howling off the abandoned buildings. Adrianne led Antoine through back alleys where things scurried away to the old harbor where the great ships used to dock, then to a place where she had been before, the City Hall that their ancestor had designed, which was now open to the elements.

They walked through the front door unhindered because no one was there. They shuffled over the tiled mosaic floors, taking a moment to stare up at the oculus, which drew in a large stream of light from above—the ceiling decorated so delicately with indented squares carved out to lessen the weight of the dome. Their steps echoed loudly in the emptiness. They slipped into a back room and then through an open door to the outside into an alley to step over the boxes and the bones from devoured chicken and through the potent stench of urine to touch a brick wall.

Hovering above was the green speck in the sky. Adrianne searched and searched for what she knew must be there from a half-memory of when she was a girl. Antoine scratched at his face, then pointed to what she was looking for—the brick marked with a "T" in black magic marker. She pushed at the third brick down. A door opened and they walked through.

"Remember this place, 'Twone, from when we were little? We used to come here with grandpapa."

"He said this was a secret place," Antoine said.

"Yes, this is a secret place."

This was the place behind the walls, behind the sky, controlling the day and the night and the wind and the rain. The hidden place maintained by The Twelve, that everyone knew about but refused to remember. They walked through the hall, past the one-way observation window where the town and the wall could be seen. Through another hall to the stairway of cinderblock walls with peeling off-white paint. These rooms were abandoned. No one should be here anymore. But they heard a noise. A shadow moved and approached them. It was Steven.

"So you've finally come," he said.

"Yes." Adrianne said. "How long have you been here?"

"Only a little while. I was waiting for you," he said. "Hi, Antoine."

Antoine bear-hugged him. When he was finally released, Steven pushed back his glasses and said, "We should go to the control room."

"Okay," Adrianne said.

They went to a room of glowing buttons and turned on the light. Steven sat at the console. The screens above showed images of every aspect of life of the world inside the city. Lessons from so long ago had taught her about the system—a privilege because of her ancestry. She and her brother were descended from the man who had designed all of this.

"Remember this place, 'Twone."

"Yeah, Adrianne, I remember," he said and sat in an office chair and swung around and around and laughed and laughed. That was indeed what they used to do when they came here all those years ago.

"The projection system has been altered in recent years, probably by the krestge. The system projects a world that people cannot escape," Steven said. "All the exits and vents have been blocked, covered from above. And there is no air flowing through to the underground."

"So what are we breathing?"

"An increasingly toxic mixture of gases made mostly of carbon dioxide."

"So we've been buried alive," Adrianne said in a voice just above a whisper.

"I've been trying to reprogram the system, but it's locked," Steven said. "As people die, they are either replaced by projections or the livable area is shrunk down to accommodate the reduced population. You, me, and Antoine are some of the last ones left."

Steven flipped a few switches, and the images on the screens changed. First the people disappeared, then the town dissolved away, then the sky. There was some movement, but mostly all was gray blackness in a cavern and a ruined underground, flooded with water in places. It was a home for the dead, a tomb.

```
** BREAK **
>>
>>
>> opendialog SECTOR: 10110001
```

: Did this really happen?

   "What?"

: Are you imagining all of this?

   "You tell me."

: I don't believe you.

   "Don't you believe your own eyes?"

: This is difficult to accept.

   "Who the hell are you anyway? And how are you in my head?"

```
: end;
>>
>> continue
```

BRIDGE PROCESS: CONTINUED

.

.

.

Steven pressed more buttons and typed at the console for a long time. Adrianne didn't want to disturb him in his work. Antoine continued to swing from side to side with his head bowed in the chair. She went to him and stopped him from moving.

"'Twone, I have to tell you something, and it's going to be hard to understand. But I need you to listen."

"What, Adrianne?" He looked worried.

"Baby," she touched his hand and said, "how do I say this? . . . Nothing in the city is real."

"What do you mean?"

"Everything and everybody. Nothing is real."

"Even Helen?"

"Even Helen."

Antoine laughed. Adrianne scrunched her face. She felt helpless. The snaking scar on his brow wiggled when he laughed, an ever-present reminder that her brother's mind was gone.

"There," Steven said. "It's done."

"What's done?" Adrianne asked.

He removed a memory card from the system and held it up for her to see. "This is the update to the Elysium system. Do you know what that is?"

"It's the archive of our people maintained in the sky in the aboveground," she replied. He placed the card into a small tube-like device and wrapped it well in plastic. Then he put it into a small duffle bag and handed it to her.

"You have to update the system."

"Me?"

"Yes, you."

"But I don't know how."

"It's not hard. Once you reach above, you place the projectile firmly on the ground facing the open sky, press the launch button, and back away. It will do the rest."

"Shouldn't you be the one to do this? You know more about it than me."

"I have to stay here in the control center. There is only one way out of the city, and that's through the water tunnels. Someone has to power down the pumping system and open the flow-ways to help you get out. It can only be controlled from here."

"But how will they get out?" She was looking at the few movements in the grayness. Adrianne felt her throat tighten. "How will you get out?"

Steven pushed back his glasses and looked away.

"There has to be another way," Adrianne said. "We can't just leave you—"

"You have to. If you don't update the system, no one will ever know what happened here."

"You and Antoine have to go," Steven said. He put something that looked like chewed gum in her hand. "Wear this in your ear. I'll direct you through the tunnels as best I can with this. Don't worry about me. I'll be all right."

Adrianne caressed Steven's face and kissed him on the forehead.

"Come on, Antoine. We need to go now."

"Where we going, Adrianne?" Antoine said.

"Above," she said. "To Elysium."

Antoine laughed.

Adrianne and Antoine walked hand in hand through the back rooms, passing bones and the decay of the ruin of their forgotten world. Adrianne thought of those who still lived in the projected town outside. Being deprived of air, they must believe themselves sickly while surrounded by fresh, healthy projections and a blue uninterrupted sky.

Steven's voice sounded in her ear, telling her where the entrance to the water tunnel stood. The opening was wide enough so that they could walk through. Antoine had to duck a little. The further they walked into the tunnel, the more flooded it became. They walked until the water came up to their waists. Steven said not to worry. He was letting the water in slowly to empty the cistern enough so that they could reach it. They would have to swim through to the other side, to where the river would be, then swim up to the top.

They followed the path of the tunnel until it reached its grated hole. The grate was easy to remove. They did it together and walked on for what felt like hours until they reached the end. Before them was a concrete basin with overflowing water.

The voice in her ear crackled and was full of static. The few words that she could make out were: "You...have...to...swim."

"Antoine, we have to jump in."

There was fear in his eyes. She reached up to touch his face and caressed the scar on his forehead, the injury that took away her brother and replaced him with this beautiful man-child. Her heart actually ached to look upon him. He stooped over her, his bulbous eyes watering with fear.

"We'll be okay," she said.

He smiled and climbed into the cistern, and she followed. They both began to swim.

The water was deep and the current swift. She felt the arms of Antoine around her, bracing her up. He was pulling her along, keeping her afloat. They moved against the flow. Above them was water and more water. She held onto him and tried to not let him go. Together they swam, hand in hand. More water. Greenish-blackness all around. Slipping. His hand, his hand, where was his hand? She floundered and searched. The instinct for air forced her upward. Up and up and up, until her head emerged into the night sky. She took in a deep breath and splashed on the surface of the water. She looked all around in the dark. She couldn't see Antoine. She couldn't feel him.

"Antoine! Antoine!"

She coughed out water. There was no answer.

She swam until she felt the dirt and rocks and pulled herself to shore. The smell of fresh air filled her lungs, and she coughed.

"Antoine! Antoine!"

Still no answer.

Adrianne prepared the device for updating the atmospheric database. She dragged herself to the shore, still calling for her brother. She removed a small rocket from her bag, set it upright on the ground, ignited its engines, and backed away. The small rocket *whooshed* into the air, higher and higher, until it disappeared from sight. The rocket burst into flame above, flowering overhead into a multitude of directions, momentarily lighting the entire sky like a giant spider's web set ablaze.

A shift in the wind. A distant heartbeat. The sound of crashing trash cans. Something was out there.

"Antoine?"

It wasn't him. It was something else. Many things. They were coming.

Adrianne ran. She ran until her lungs burned. And all the while she kept calling his name.

"Antoine! Antoine!"

Adrianne was running and calling and running and calling. She ran so fast nothing could catch her. She ran and soared up into the air far toward the horizon. She was the wind. She took flight. She passed through a haze of green, and the land of darkness gave way to trees and a blue sky.

This was Elysium. This was Earth. This was home.

21.

Floating high above a place long healed from the dust and the mist. Dipping and swooping through the valleys of a land very much like paradise. Alighting on the branch of a tree to look down upon the inhabitants below. Watching, seeing, learning. A cool wind carried the overwhelming scent of pine. And there was silence, except for the occasional chirp or squawk from a bird and the flutter flutter of wings as an owl rustled the leaves. A group of rabbits huddled in the bushes, some of them digging their way into a new home.

A herd of elk passed. One stopped to chew on a leaf. Its antlers rose high upon its elegant head, spreading upwards like giant fingers into a crown. It spied Adrianne sitting against the trunk of a tree. It looked at her. The others continued on their path, uninterested. And soon the last elk, too, left to follow its herd.

Adrianne breathed deeply, feeling an ache in her lungs. She coughed and wiped her lips with her hand. Blood appeared on her fingers. She wiped them on the tree behind her, feeling its rough bark. The blood came off and disappeared into nothing.

A rustle in the trees. Adrianne tried to move, but her legs wouldn't respond. The lower half of her body felt numb, as if it didn't belong to her. She was helpless. Closing her eyes, she coughed again and waited.

The clock in her mind calculated minutes. It felt like hours. She could see something moving toward her. Its slow, light crunch over the twigs and dead leaves sounded as if it had the weight of a child. The bulky, weightless four-dimensional creature was much larger than that.

It stopped five or six feet away from her. Adrianne couldn't see its eyes. The krestge had no eyes. But she could feel it looking at her. Its planar shifts made it more shadow than form. It breathed deeply. Adrianne was too weak to stand. Too tired. Too worn out.

With her head bent, she waited for it to do whatever it was going to do. There was a long moment of silence. She faced it when it stood over her. To her surprise, the presence of the thing elicited not fear, but curiosity.

"Who are you?" she said.

A hawk cried from above, almost in answer.

"My~~name is~~~Tkeclc Zinn."

Its voice rippled in the air like an echoing distant vibration.

"I was born~~on this world and raised~~in a small vill-age not~~far from this meadow. I am a~~research-er and I've been~~~look-ing into the history~~of the found-ing of~~our col-on-ies here.~~"

So they live here now, Adrianne thought. It was what she had long suspected was their ultimate goal.

It continued, "I dis-covered~~your program run-ning~~~in the at-mos-phere . . . I was~~ surprised to find~~such a thing."

"It wasn't meant for the likes of you."

"I~~un-der-stand~~your anger."

It moved, and the air around it shimmered in a strange way, a shadow dancing on light. It had more than length and height and depth, it seemed to reach around itself, moving in and out of step with itself. Adrianne perceived that she was seeing it on all sides. It held something familiar in what Adrianne supposed were its hands. It was her portable console. Zinn laid it down on the ground next to her.

"I tried~~to fix this~~," Zinn said.

It was rusted through, beyond repair.

"This can't be fixed."

"So~~it would seem."

Adrianne rubbed a stray eyelash out of her eye and brushed it away.

"~~Would you~~like to stand?"

Adrianne thought for a moment then said, "I can't. I'm broken."

"I may~~have dam-aged some of~~your data files~~~with my bridge pro-gram.~~For this, I apo-lo-gize.~~~~May-be I can help. I still have~~some mea-sure~~of control to con-nect~~~into your systems."

She felt a sudden jolt and the numbness in her legs released. "There," it said.

"Yes," Adrianne said and located the access point from which the alien had gained entry and closed it.

"~~Please, come.~~I want to show~~~you something."

Adrianne braced herself against the tree. Her hand touched the surface of the tree, and yet not. The air filled her lungs, and yet not. The sun warmed her face, the heat was there, and yet not.

The krestge moved off, twisting within itself. It stopped several times and turned to see if Adrianne followed. It was an eerie sight to watch something move and remain still at the same time. Yet Adrianne continued to follow.

All around her was green and alive. A large flock of birds crossed the sky, momentarily blocking out the sun. The sounds of creatures both great and small made the chorus of a song with the wind rustling through the leaves forming the melody. They approached a small brook. Adrianne bent down to touch the flowing water. It went through her hand.

Beyond the water, beyond the canopy of trees, a cluster of shimmering towers made of something akin to silver rose into the air. They seemed to float rather than sit on the ground. Adrianne remained still and took in the sight. The towers were like Zinn; she could see all sides of them. Her mind told her that this was impossible, and yet that was what her eyes perceived. They seemed both beautiful and sinister.

"~~This is our~~cap-i-tal on Earth~~~and it is my home."

"I see."

Adrianne closed her eyes and calculated. She knew where she was. This is where it had all happened. This was where her city once was. This was home.

"All that you~~exper-ienced~~hap-pened a long, long time ago.~~~It is a for-got-ten history.~~The story of hu-mans~~living here before us~~is not one we are told.~~If I had not seen~~the evidence myself,~~I'm not sure that~~~I would have be-lieved..."

Adrianne felt weak. She found a large rock to sit on, took off her nonexistent shoes, and put her feet into the water. It flowed though her as if she were a specter. Her clothes and her body were fading as if being absorbed by the air.

"It is clear~~to me that~~a great crime has been~~~done to your people," Zinn said. "I swear to you,~~~I will not rest un-til the truth~~of what hap-pened here~~~is re-vealed."

Adrianne closed her eyes then said, "So, we are all dead."

"No, your people~~that es-caped in ships ar-rived~~safely on that other~~~world. They live and thrive~~there to this day."

His planar sheets shifted and shadows flowed over his outer shell.

"Where is Antoine?"

Tkeclc made a sound that was something like a groan.

"Where is he?"

After a long silence Zinn answered, "~~He is like your-self,~~a memory writ-ten~~~in the sky."

The air moved against her skin, then through her fading body. Her hands were numbing and her fingertips tingled. A flutter in her systems triggered a Level 2 warning. She adjusted her pathways and brushed away a tear.

Adrianne decided what must be done. What was life without someone to love? She finished adjusting the locks on her systems. It would take a human hand to open them again.

"I would still~~like to learn~~~more," Zinn said.

"I'm sorry, but this information was not for you."

"I~~meant you~~~no harm."

"I know," Adrianne said.

Passing the krestge, Adrianne left the water to lie down on the grasses beside the brook, which opened to a field of sweet scented wildflowers of pink and yellow. She was becoming translucent, no more than an apparition, a ghost of the past. Many things drifted through her mind as it was shutting down, mostly the memory of Antoine floating somewhere in the heavens—her always companion, her friend, her lover, her brother, her father, her son. *Antoine.*

She looked up into the blue, blue and felt the warmth of the sun shining through the clouds and said, "I would like to have seen him once again. He was so beautiful."

Then her eyes closed, and she whispered, "End Program."

```
** PROGRAM END **

>>
>> close bridge
disconnecting...

*BRIDGE DISCONNECTED*
.
.
.
```

Hadrian and Antinous

During his reign, the Emperor Hadrian (76 AD – 138 AD) had Rome in a constant state of construction. Among his many projects were the Pantheon and the Temple of Venus, the largest temple in ancient Rome. He is most famously remembered for the great wall he built across Britain—Hadrian's Wall—made to keep the barbarians at bay.

In those days it was not unusual for an older man of great political stature to take a young male lover. And so Hadrian loved the young and beautiful Antinous (c. 111 AD – 130 AD), who would probably have been in his late teens when their relationship began. Antinous was known to have a quick wit to match his beauty. Possibly that is what first attracted Hadrian's attention. In any case, the pair traveled all across the Roman world together. They liked to ride and hunt and have long lavish parties where wine and conversation with like-minded individuals were the main entertainment.

While in Egypt, Hadrian took ill, and Antinous went on a boat ride without him. There Antinous fell into the river Nile and drowned. It may have been an accident. Some speculate that Antinous committed suicide as a sacrifice to save Hadrian's life since he was sick. Or maybe Antinous was murdered to avoid the shame for Hadrian were they to continue their relationship past the time it was considered appropriate. (A relationship such as this was thought proper to end once the boy began to show facial hair.) Whichever the case, what happened next is not in dispute. After Hadrian was told of Antinous' death, he went into a fit of mourning so severe that it made those around him fear for his sanity. He never forgot Antinous. On the contrary, Hadrian did what he knew how to do best—he built things. Monument after monument after monument was constructed in memory of Antinous. Busts, statues, coins, even towns, cities, and rivers were named after him. Over and over again, the image of Antinous could be found everywhere. Antinous was also deified by the Egyptians, as those who died in the Nile often were. Perhaps this was also a gift for the grief-stricken emperor.

Hadrian had the constellation Ganymede renamed after Antinous, so that even the stars were marked in remembrance of the one he loved. The constellation above it was Aquila, the eagle. (In the Greek myth, Zeus turned into an eagle and stole Ganymede, bringing him to Mount Olympus.) Thus Hadrian was placing himself as the great bird so that the pair could be seen forever together in the night sky: Aquila with its wings outstretched carrying the young Antinous up towards the heavens.

Acknowledgements

There are so many people to thank who have helped, encouraged, and loved me along this writer's journey: Djibril al-Ayad, Pierre Bennu, K Tempest Bradford, Gail Cruise-Roberson, John DeNardo, Minister Faust, Jeffrey Ford, Andrea Hairston and Pan Morgan, Buzz Harris, Mary Frances Hatfield, N.K. Jemisin, Reid MacDonald (your beta read feedback was fabulous!), J.M. McDermott, my awesome agent Kristopher O'Higgins, the NAACP ACT-SO program, Budd Parr, Edwin Raynor, Marguerite Reed, Alta Starr (for giving me my first real book when I was thirteen "I Love Myself When I'm Laughing" A Zora Neale Hurston Reader), the Stonecoast MFA Program in Creative Writing especially my Stonecoast mentors James Patrick Kelly, David Anthony Durham, Ted Deppe, and Elizabeth Hand (You guys are the BEST! *Mwah*) and also Patricia Smith & Tim Seibles (for teaching me how to read in public), Rozanna Tendler (rest in peace, girl), Sheree Renée Thomas, L Timmel Duchamp and Kathryn Wilham, Jeff VanderMeer, Ms. Kathleen Walcott, Saul Williams (for the use of his wonderful poem), My WisCon family, and for their writerly inspiration: Sherman Alexie, James Baldwin, Octavia E. Butler, Ursula Le Guin, Ha Jin, Toni Morrison, and Gloria Naylor.

And above everyone else, Geoff Wisner my life partner with whom I've traveled this long and tough and beautiful road. You are the beat in my heart and I love you so very, very much.

Author Biography

A Jamaican-British American (born in London, England), Jennifer Marie Brissett came to the US when she was four and grew up in Cambridge, MA. She was a software engineer and web developer for many years before she moved to Brooklyn, NY, to build the indie bookstore Indigo Café & Books, which she ran for three and a half years.

Jenn has a Master's in Creative Writing from the Stonecoast MFA Program at the University of Southern Maine, concentrating in Speculative Fiction, and a Bachelor's in Interdisciplinary Engineering (Electrical Engineering with a concentration in Visual Art) from Boston University. She is a writer and sometimes artist who has had a few shows in cafes in the Boston area.

Her stories can be found in *Morpheus Tales*, *Warrior Wisewoman 2*, *The Future Fire*, *Thaumatrope*, and *Halfway Down the Stairs*, where her work was nominated for the *Dzanc Best of the Web* series, included in *The Best of Halfway Down the Stairs, 2005-2010*, and a finalist for the 2013 *storySouth* Million Writers Award.

She lives in New York City with her husband, where they both fully accept that their cat rules the house. Her website can be found at www.jennbrissett.com.